For Jen – 24/10/2014

Three Cubic Feet

Thanks so much for coming out today – lovely to meet you at Bath Spa U!

Best,

[illegible]

a novella by

Lania Knight

Mint Hill Books
Main Street Rag Publishing Company
Charlotte, North Carolina

Author photo: Don Shrubshell/*Columbia Daily Tribune*

Acknowledgements:

Portions of an early version of this book were published in *42opus* as a short story, "Into Her Mess."

Library of Congress Control Number: 2012935445

ISBN: 978-1-59948-363-4

Produced in the United States of America

Mint Hill Books
PO Box 690100
Charlotte, NC 28227
www.MainStreetRag.com

for Jeff

CONTENTS

I don't know why I'm a one man guy
Or why this is a one man show
But these three cubic feet of bone and blood and meat
Are what I love and know

—Loudon Wainwright III
"One Man Guy," *I'm Alright*

CHAPTER ONE

My dad and I both stare at the rain fly stretched between our hands, its strange angles refusing to be reduced to a simple square. "Okay, Son, let's fold this thing," Dad says. He gives it a shake. "Matt had the right idea." We stand there a moment, and he releases one corner of the rain fly to scratch beneath his faded Hawaiian shirt. Then he is immobile, thinking. "We could be home by now," he says.

"Right—" My voice is nearly steady. "We're doing the whole drive today?"

Dad lets go of the rain fly and mumbles something.

I hum to keep from speaking. I fold, alone, and then I begin unhooking each pole from the tent, pushing the tubes through the pockets along the seams.

"Too bad you can't help drive, Theo."

That tight thing starts up in my stomach, the thing that doesn't go away until I can be by myself. I toss the bundle of tent poles to the ground.

He watches me. "You aren't… Don't tell me you had a birthday."

"Okay. I won't," I say.

"Did you, Theo?"

"Well. Yeah, Dad, I did."

He takes off his glasses, and I look at the scar below his eye, the one that's curved just the same way his glasses are curved, the scar he got from the car accident that almost killed him eleven months ago. He wipes his forehead on his shirtsleeve and then cleans his glasses in little circular motions, squinting.

They all forgot my sixteenth birthday.

I start folding the tent by myself while my little sister Samantha and her best friend Kate argue about their swimsuits. Della, my step-mom, stands at the propane stove perched on the end of the picnic table, stirring the oatmeal, telling the girls to be nice. I'm ready to leave and be the person behind the steering wheel. I need to practice. Florida is almost over, and four states away, my best friend, Jonathan, is waiting back home in Missouri.

"Speed it up, you two!" Della calls out. "Breakfast is ready!"

My dad looks toward the picnic table, in a daze. He stretches with his hands on his lower back and pulls up one knee, then the other, leaning against a tree to keep his balance as each foot lifts five, six, seven seconds. The pain migrates across his face, escapes his mouth with a low groan. But he doesn't complain. He is alive, and that is enough. "You'd better eat while you've got the chance," he tells me.

I can't be angry with him for not remembering my birthday, for not making things right. I start folding the camo-green tarp, and he finds his cane and shuffles away.

"Where are you going?" Della calls after him, and he waves her off with his free hand. She turns to me. "Let's eat," she says.

I gather up our folded camping equipment and watch my dad disappear on the other side of a rise, drifting among the palmetto bushes and live oaks of the surrounding campsites. "Alright," I say.

Della isn't really my mother. My mom was the plump, huggable type. Della is skinny, and she teaches junior high math. My mom was a botanical illustrator, an artist. She died of breast cancer when I was six. She was still nursing my little sister Samantha. I remember what it felt like. I remember hating the baby girl in mom's arms, thinking Samantha gave my mom the cancer. The last real memory I have of Mom is her body, shrunken up like a bird, swallowed whole on the queen-sized bed Sam sometimes still got to sleep in. Everything hurt when I touched Mom, even when I just touched the old quilt she kept folded at the foot of the bed. Every bone in her body ached, she told me. So I didn't touch her, even to hold her hand and say goodbye when Dad told me it was time. Of course, that was stupid and selfish of me, but I was only six years old.

I wedge against the van, alone for a minute, holding the tarp, tent and rain fly to my chest. A breeze stirs the needles of the jack pines nearby, ruffling the surface of the pool of water at the base of the trees' roots. I inherited all of Mom's plant taxonomies when she died, so I know the names of all the trees and bushes and flowers from here to the Ozarks in Missouri. I can't help but notice the plants, their names popping into my head without my asking them to.

I'm tired. I open up the car top carrier, put our stuff inside, and then look in my backpack for *Heart of Darkness*, the book I have to read for British Literature. I stare at the cover and think of Matt, the new instructor in Dad's department at Missouri State, how he stopped at our campsite on his way out yesterday. I was sitting in the hammock reading my book when he shook my dad's hand through the car window. Matt looked at me. He waved and said something like *Take it easy*. I said *Sure* and watched him drive away.

I wish Della had never invited him on this trip. So what if he's new and lonely.

"Would you stop already?" Della says. She is standing behind me, holding a steaming bowl of oatmeal. She is standing too close, and her presence feels like the confinement of a short, choking leash. The closer she gets, the more I know that she will be the one to figure out what I did to Matt. I take the oatmeal from her and eat it and try not to puke it up.

Later, after we say goodbye to all of the families who traveled here with us from Missouri and who are now ready to leave for home before we are, after we stuff every last cooking utensil and dirty sock into the van, I decide to remind Della that I need to log more hours of practice driving.

She tells the girls they can go play one last time at the beach, and then I drop it on her. "Do you think I could drive home?" I say.

"Oh God," she says. "Your birthday."

The tears well up instantly and spill over.

"I'll make it up to you," she says. She touches my shoulder—I let her—and she hands me the keys. She doesn't like making mistakes.

When the girls come back from their last swim and Dad returns from his shuffle around the campground, I drive. For many, many hours, I drive. I pull away from our campsite, the last coals in the fire ring sending up white tufts of smoke, and soon the black asphalt camp road is replaced by concrete ticking beneath our tires. We make our way west from Florida to Alabama and then up the long, straight highway leading north through Mississippi, only taking one break for gas. Longleaf pines crawl by on either side. There isn't any decent music on the radio, but I leave the dial tuned to an oldies station. That only holds off Della for a little while. She looks back between the seats to see what I already noticed in the rearview mirror—my dad, Samantha, and Kate are all asleep.

"Maybe you should take your driver's test when we get back home." She has apologized a thousand times about my birthday.

"Sure," I say. I've had my permit for six months, but with all of Dad's surgeries and physical therapy, no matter what I ask, Della says *not now*. But things are changing.

She rolls down the window and swings the visor around to block the late morning sun. "I was surprised Matt went home a day early," she says.

It takes much effort not to respond. I sing along with Van Morrison. Brown-eyed Girl. Dad's favorite.

Della turns a few more pages of the magazine on her lap. "Weren't you surprised he left yesterday?" She knows I'm gay. Dad knows. But no one knows about Matt. Yet.

"I guess so," I say. I drum my fingers during the horn section.

"Did he say anything to you? What about when you rode into town with him?"

"It's not like we had some big conversation."

Actually, we did. It was two days ago, on my birthday.

Della reaches for her water bottle in the cup holder, untwists the lid and then takes a long drink. "He didn't say how things were going with his daughters or anything?"

I focus on staying in my lane when the blow-by from a big truck shakes the minivan.

Matt's girls were supposed to come with him to Florida, but Matt's ex-wife said no, she wanted them to spend the break with her, and Matt had given in.

Della closes the bottle and puts it away.

"Guys don't talk about things like that, not like girls do."

"You don't have to be a girl to want to talk about things. Are you sure there isn't something—"

"Nothing happened."

She keeps rearranging her legs, folding one under the other and leaning on the armrest toward me.

My hands are tight on the steering wheel.

Yes, I drove Matt's car on my birthday.

It's like this: late in the afternoon, I go with him into town. He is buying more beer for the adults, and I am buying a new flashlight for my turd little sister.

At the grocery store, Matt and I separate inside the entrance. I push a cart and take my time staring at the displays, wondering what kind of food Matt likes. In the parking lot, Matt is waiting in the car, on the passenger's side.

"What's up?" I say.

"I was thinking you might want to drive us back to the campground," Matt answers.

"I don't have a license."

"You have a permit, don't you?"

I stand up and look around the parking lot. My hands are damp. I sit in the driver's seat. It is just slightly too far back, and I consider not moving it forward, but safety wins out over pride. Not until I rest my hand on the gearshift do I realize that Matt's little blue hatchback isn't an automatic. Jonathan, my best friend back home, taught me how to drive a stick shift. I just have to breathe.

The gears don't grind and the car doesn't die at stoplights. I follow the highway through town that leads back to camp while Matt looks at my *Men's Health and Fitness* magazine. He asks if I am looking for a new workout routine, but I say no. "I don't get it for the workout suggestions," I tell him.

Matt knows I like men.

When I babysat for him once, I stayed at his house awhile after he got home. He played banjo and talked about a Civil War reenactment of a rendezvous in the Ozark Mountains. He told me about his dad, a Civil War buff, and then played a few songs for me and asked about my schoolwork, my friends, my girlfriend. Usually, I don't reveal myself, but with Matt, I couldn't tell a lie. I wanted him to like me, who I really am, not who I pretend to be at school.

But on the way to the campground, Matt stares out the car window, at the hotels and condos and dunes passing by. He is lightly stoned. I smelled it when I got in the car, but I don't say anything. Matt starts talking about some old Soloflex ads of a guy taking off his shirt. "You can't see his face," Matt says. "All you can see are his abs and his arms. Because the shirt is covering his head."

I don't know what he's talking about. I don't say anything. I just drive. Those painted lines on the road are so close together. Too close. And I love hearing Matt talk about guys.

When I finally speak, the sun has dropped to the horizon directly ahead of us, swelling to a brilliant watery red around the edges. White rolling sand dunes studded with beach tea bushes and swaying oat grass stretch out on each side of the road. There is no shoulder. Dipping lower and lower until it is swallowed by the horizon, the sun winks out.

"Do you know about the flashlight tour of Fort Pickens?" I ask.

"I'm going," Matt says, "But it's creepy." He tells me about a book he found in the gift shop. "All of these black and white photos of dead Civil War soldiers," he says, "strewn across fields, left near the bases of trees. The photographers actually arranged the bodies for more dramatic effect."

"That's weirder than reenactment?"

"Sure," Matt says. His voice gets quiet. "Maybe it's a fascination people have with what they don't understand. Take enough pictures of death, or grief… maybe you'll find some answer you didn't have before. It's disrespectful. A private moment. A dead man can't turn the photographer away."

My hands tremble. I know Matt is stoned. I've been around enough people who smoke to know that sometimes they just ramble and don't make a lot of sense. But what is spooky is that it's like a conversation I might have had with my dad. Before. But Matt is not like my dad. I don't want to talk about death, but Matt keeps on. "Photographers took pictures of dead people during the Victorian era as a way of paying homage and remembering them," he says. "It wasn't creepy to them like it is to us now. It was normal. Strange how things like that could change. Now, it's an invasion of something sacred," Matt says. "All of the choice lies entirely in the hands of the photographer."

As Matt speaks, I imagine my dad smashed inside his truck after the accident, his head turned at an odd angle so that his bloody face can be captured by a camera lens, and I grip the steering wheel tightly, trying to force the photograph of my father—dead—out of my head.

"It looks like they're sleeping," Matt says, "the Victorian images of the dead. But the soldiers, you *know* they're not sleeping." Matt is quiet for a moment.

"When I first saw my dad after the accident," I tell him, "his head was bandaged and they had these things on his feet that kept inflating."

Matt is silent.

I can't stop. "These bags on his feet would fill with air all of a sudden and his whole body would jerk. Like he was trying to fall asleep and they wouldn't let him." I stare at the road. "His legs were crushed and his blood wouldn't circulate on its own. They had to re-break his knees after they healed. And they'll probably do it again." I twitch. I wipe one of my palms on my shorts, then the other. My dad's brow and nose were so swollen that part of his face nearly lifted itself through the bandaging, like someone had jammed a wooden cross up under the gauze. And he moaned. Every time the machine would make the cuffs on his feet suddenly inflate, he would jump and moan.

I have dreams, nightmares, of what my dad's face looked like under the gauze, one of the lenses of his eyeglasses shoved into his eye socket. It's like this: I'm lying on a steel operating table in a one-room stone castle. There is a twenty-foot high chain-link fence just outside. My dad, his body battered by the accident, is hiding beneath me, under the metal table. When there are no guards around, I help my dad outside the castle and over the fence, knowing that I can't climb it myself. When I get back to the table, I fall asleep, but then I wake later, panicked, minus both my legs and my left arm. I lie on the table for hours, thinking I will lose my right arm too, but then I fall asleep waiting.

But Della is still talking. I'm not with Matt. I'm not dreaming.

"...some offhand comments about his ex-wife," she says.

Matt's ex-wife.

"It's been a long time since you and I have had a serious talk."

"About what?" I say. She is digging for something.

She takes a deep breath, leaning too close. "I realize I've been letting a lot of things go because of your dad..." She looks at me. "Theo, I want you to tell me if you're in a relationship."

"What?"

"I mean a physical relationship with a boy."

I keep my eyes straight ahead. "Look, Della. Everything's fine. I've got friends. My schoolwork is going okay." I look at her. "Coach says my running is fine—I'm having a great season."

"Theo, you never go out, the only friend you have is Jonathan, and you've been nothing but sullen and distant this entire trip."

"I'm a teenager," I say. My jaw is fucking tight. "And you forgot my birthday."

My little sister calls from the back, and Della stretches around to look. "What is it, Hon?" she says, and then tells Sam we'll stop at the next rest area. "I'm sorry," Della says to me in a low voice, still leaning across the armrest. "If there is ever anything you need to talk about, I'm here."

It's almost two in the morning when we turn onto our street. Jonathan's house is next door. Jonathan's old house. He and his family didn't come to Florida for spring break this year because they had to stay home all week and move their shit to a big house on a wooded lot south of town.

Darkness clings to the street, and Jonathan's truck isn't parked near the curb in its usual spot. A realtor's sign glows faintly in the corner of his yard, reflecting a distant light. I can't help staring at the empty windows of Jonathan's house each time I pass with another armful of gear. I washed every one of those windows with Jonathan last summer.

It was like this: Dr. Norton, Jonathan's dad, offered to pay us both for washing windows. Later in the summer, Jonathan's soccer ball shattered the picture window in the living room. The replacement sucked up all of our money plus every last bit of Jonathan's savings. It was my kick that did the damage, but Jonathan took the blame. He knew his dad was a hot-headed motherfucker, and he didn't want me to get hurt.

He didn't want me to get hurt.

My dad and I carry the camping gear to the garage while Della helps the girls to bed. Dad says his knees are aching after sitting all day in the van. It's cold, and his breath comes out in steamy puffs. With each armload he walks less and less steadily.

"I'll get the rest," I say and finish unloading. I go to my room and shut the door before Della tries to find me.

I sit on the edge of my bed with my head in my hands until I remember the shells I put in my swim trunks. I dig around in my backpack, feeling for the fabric with my fingertips. There are five shells—I set them on my nightstand. I lean back and slide my legs between my favorite blue flannel sheets. I want to call Jonathan, to find out what happened with the new kid, Richard, to tell Jonathan every stupid thing that happened with Matt at the fort the night of my birthday. The kiss. The blowjob. Running on the beach afterwards wishing I could swim out too far.

CHAPTER TWO

Sunlight slants through the blinds, illuminating my Greg Louganis poster of a downward spiral into an aquamarine Olympic-sized pool. A Rufus Wainwright CD cover is tacked on the wall alongside Greg's fantastic dive. Near the window is a movie-sized poster of painted red lips cradling a cross-dressed Tim Curry and dripping letters that spell out *Rocky Horror Picture Show*. Below it is John Cameron Mitchell swinging a head-full of yellow hair as Hedwig of *Hedwig and the Angry Inch*. Hanging just under my bottom shelf is my grandfather's gold pocket watch, an old-time locomotive etched on its surface.

"Theo, wake up."

I am awake, and I watch the doorknob jiggle.

"Let me in, Bitch, or I'll have to break this door down."

"I'm not letting you in," I say, but I unlock the door. Jonathan shoves it open.

"Come in, Asshole."

"Did I hurt you?" Jonathan takes my wrist and rotates my hand a few times. "There. How's that?"

"Great."

"How was the trip? I thought you wouldn't be back until tonight." Jonathan pulls the chair from my desk and sits in it, tilting back with his feet on my bed.

His shoes are at the front door in accordance with Della's command. "Those better be clean socks," I say, grouchier than I feel. I shake out my hand.

Jonathan's dark hair spikes out from under his knit cap, and week-old stubble has grown along his chin. He pulls one foot to his nose, balancing with the other. He takes in a deep breath. "They're clean." He puts his sock-covered toes back on the bed. "Now, tell me about Florida."

I lean against the wall. I pull the pillow onto my lap, and I stare at Jonathan. "You first."

"Why," Jonathan says in a high, feminine voice, "I thought you might have forgotten our little bet." He flutters his hand as if he were waving a fan.

"Did I win?" I ask.

"Ah." He lowers his voice. "I still don't know." He presses his palm into his toes, cracking several of them. "He helped me move. I brought him out for a burger. Maybe, but I don't think so." Jonathan isn't ready to tell me the truth. Richard is gay. I caught the kid looking at me too long, avoiding all talk of girls, and of course, there is the choker at his neck. But Jonathan ignores it all. Richard is new. He's from Chicago, not this bullshit Bible Belt town of Springfield, Missouri. Either Jonathan is clueless or he's trying to protect me.

"So I win," I say.

"For now. Since I don't know otherwise, we'll assume he's gay." He shifts his feet and starts cracking his other toes. "Now tell me about Florida. What about that tour guide with the moustache?"

"No." Last year, Jonathan had a crush on the guy with the moustache, and the year before that, the blond ex-football player.

Jonathan reaches over to the desk and picks up one of the shells. "These are sweet." He runs a flat pink shell between each of his fingers, like he is performing a card trick. "You brought these back for me, right?"

"Maybe."

"Did you miss me?"

"No."

"Good, I didn't miss you either." He looks down at the shell in his palm. "Someone gave you these. You met someone on the beach, didn't you?"

"No."

He squints at me and crosses his arms over his chest. "What about that new guy?"

"What about him?"

Jonathan drops the front legs of the chair to the floor. "You'd better tell me everything."

"There's nothing to tell."

"Bitch," Jonathan leans forward, elbows on his knees. "I know you better than that."

I look down at my lap. I wrap the edge of the pillowcase around my index finger. Then Jonathan yanks it away.

"Cut it out!"

"Alright," he says. "I'm not leaving until you 'fess up."

I scratch behind my ears and wait. No, I can't press for details about Richard, but it's not a problem for Jonathan to keep asking about Matt. "I fucked up." I look at him. "I really fucked up."

"What'd you do?"

It was my fault. If we hadn't gotten into that stupid argument. "That short woman with the one arm lead the flashlight tour. She talked a lot about Geronimo."

"Only important details, please."

"Matt—the new instructor—we were near the back. Looking at those excavated arches by the old cannons. His flashlight was running out." I take back the pillow and tangle my hands in the pillowcase. "I tried to give Matt my flashlight. The tour group moved on and he and I kept hanging back. Every twenty feet or so, these doorways opened up in the wall. They lead to the low hallways where they used to store munitions."

"I remember," Jonathan says.

It's like this: I duck inside one of the low doorways. I ask Matt to join me.

He says no.

"We've got time," I say.

Matt holds my arm, and then lets go.

"It doesn't go back that far."

"No," he says.

I come out of the tunnel and stare into Matt's face. Shadows. He's at least an inch taller than I am, maybe two. And he is standing very close. I give him my flashlight. He takes it, and then he pushes my hand to the side. I don't move.

He says, "Theo, I can't." My armpits tingle. He is running his hand through his hair. "I don't like tunnels," he says, trying to walk around me. "We should go," he says.

"Matt, I didn't mean—"

"Take it." He holds out my flashlight.

"There's plenty of moonlight."

"You could get lost."

"I won't get lost," I say.

I'm walking along dark corridors, my sense of direction gone. I wait in a doorway and hear his footsteps.

"You should come back to camp with me."

"I'm alright."

"Your parents will worry."

"I can take care of myself."

"If I show up without you, your parents will ask questions."

My feet won't move. "Tell them you didn't see me."

"There's no moon." He looks at the sky. "Here."

I reach for the light, but I grab his hand.

"I kissed him." I'm staring at my hands. "I kissed him."

"Serious?" Jonathan's voice is a whisper.

"And he kissed me back."

I hold Matt's jaw. He tries to push me away. Then I slide one hand to his waist and the other to cup the base of his skull. He struggles. Then he stops.

"I went down on him." I look at Jonathan, steady blue eyes, still, quiet hands. "I unbuttoned his pants. I told him it was my birthday." I stare into Jonathan's eyes. "I told him the only thing I wanted was him. And he let me."

It's my first time. My first blowjob. I don't know if I can take him all the way in, but I do. He tastes like saltwater and sweat and the flesh of ripe fruit. He can't stop shaking after the orgasm. I put my arm around him. *Would you go down on me?* He wraps his arms around my waist, but then his body freezes.

"He's your first head!" Jonathan says.

"Stop," I say. "I fucked up, okay?"

He sits back down. He leans forward. "What?" he says.

"We just stood there," I say. I look past his shoulder at the bare branches on the tree outside the window.

"Yeah?" Jonathan says.

"I was trying…" I roll my head side to side against the wall. I look at the pocket watch, at the stacks of CD's on the shelves above.

Jonathan puts his chair flat on the floor again. "Just say it."

"I was still so fucking jazzed. I should have just walked away." I wait. "At first, it was no big deal. I mean, we were just hugging, and I thought everything was okay. Like, he got through being freaked out, and we were holding each other, and then…" I can't keep talking. Is Jonathan jealous? Am I an ass?

"Yes?" Jonathan leans forward. "I'm listening, okay? Just tell me."

"He started crying. And he was yelling. He had a hold of my shirt. And then I left."

"You left?" Jonathan's eyes tighten.

"Yeah, I left," I say, but Jonathan keeps asking me questions. I'm trying to leave out the part about shoving Matt against the bricks. The part about us fighting.

He is shaking me. He has my shoulders. I push him. His head hits the wall. It doesn't knock him out or anything. He slides down to the floor and screams at me to *get the fuck away*. I run to the beach. I have to get away. He leaves the next morning. *Take it easy*, he says.

Jonathan raises his arms and puts his hands behind his head. His feet are back on the edge of my bed and he's pushing against it, slowly rocking. The shell is in his lap.

"Heavy."

"Yeah."

Jonathan picks up another shell from my desk. It's a conical-shaped bone-colored spiral. He rolls it between his fingers and then lays it across the other shell on his lap. I stare at it, remembering the tee shirt he bought me in Florida last year—a tight pink tank top that says "Everything's Better on the Beach." It's buried in the back of my closet. Jonathan is into guys like I am, but he won't do anything with me. He says he won't increase my risk factor. But I think he just isn't into me.

"Forget about it. You'll see him somewhere, you'll feel like a freak, and then it will pass."

"I can't forget about it."

"Let it rest for a few days. We'll figure something out."

"We?"

"Of course. You think I'd leave you on your own?"

I hug my knees. "My parents suspect something," I say. "Della kept asking questions on the drive home. About Matt. You. If I've had any 'physical' relationships."

Jonathan sets the shells back on the desk and lets his chair sit level on the floor again. He rubs his hands across his thighs and looks at me. "You need to be carful. We'll come up with something. Stay relaxed. Think like an innocent man."

"Fuck that."

"Really. Come see our new house. Let's go out tonight and celebrate your birthday. There's a place downtown I've been wanting to bring you for months."

"I don't want to go to a gay bar for my birthday."

"What did your parents get you?"

"Didn't you hear me? Everyone forgot."

Jonathan laughs. "Come on, they were just distracted. Your dad's still recovering, and Della is a bitch."

"Whatever."

He leaps out of the chair and pounces on me, pinning me on the bed. "You don't need a birthday spanking, do you?" He likes to play like this.

"No," I say, struggling, and I see the clock. It's almost noon.

"Shove some shit in a bag and take a shower at my house," he says. He rolls over on the bed and leans against the wall. I gather up my stuff, and he stands and stretches, touching his hands to the highest shelf. "Since when did you start listening to Brazilian music?" He takes down a jewel case to read the front insert. "You thinking of running away to Brazil?"

"Maybe."

"You'd have to learn Portuguese."

If that's what it takes to get away from this ridiculous family, maybe I'll learn Portuguese. "Here," I say, sliding the shells off the desk onto Jonathan's open hand. "These are for you."

"Theo, you shouldn't have." He sets the CD case on the desk and takes the shells. "Your birthday present is at my house," he says. He spreads the shells on his palm and turns each one over, then folds them into his hand, and in a more serious voice, says thanks. He puts the shells in his pocket and stands at the door, his hand on the knob. "This Matt motherfucker is going to pay."

For the first time in days, the tension in my gut begins to unwind. "It's my fight, Jonathan."

"You don't have to do it alone."

"Do *what*?"

"That's what I'm talking about. You need me."

Yeah, I need you.

He laughs and I close the door behind us.

Jonathan waits for me outside. In the kitchen, Dad is sitting at the counter on a wooden stool.

"Hey, Dad."

"Son." He nods. He turns the paper to the Saturday sports section. He wobbles, and then sticks his leg out to balance. "Shit," he says.

I scan the counter for food. There's a fading apple in the bowl on the center island countertop. "Jonathan wants me to go over to his house."

"The new house?" Dad rustles the pages, turning from national sports to his favorite, the college scores.

"Yeah," I say through a mouthful of mealy apple. I check the date on the jug of skim milk. "Any good news?"

"Nope," Dad says and sets the paper next to his mug. "Damn if I didn't miss some of March Madness again." He takes a sip of coffee and looks out the kitchen window, rubbing his neck. "Looks empty."

"Their new place is supposed to be nice—way out in the woods." I grab some toaster pastries from the pantry and shove them in my pocket. "So, it's alright if I go to Jonathan's?"

"Wait." He lifts the other sections of the newspaper, looking for something. "Della left you a note." It's a lavender sheet from her memo pad.

I read it and put the milk back in the refrigerator. I shut the door too hard. "Come on, Dad. Help me out." She wants me to take all of the sleeping bags and wash them in the triple size washers at the laundromat. There's a roll of quarters by the microwave.

"I've got my own list." He rubs the spot between his eyebrows and pushes another lavender note to the edge of the counter. Della's angular writing covers the slip of paper.

"Can't you tell her I'll do it tomorrow?"

Dad closes the paper and folds all of the sections together. "You know she doesn't listen to me." He taps his head. "Not since the old noggin got whacked."

Okay, it's an attempt at being funny.

He looks at my backpack. "Why the bag?"

"Extra clothes in case Jonathan and I go out tonight."

"Just don't come home too late."

"I'll probably sleep over."

Dad follows me as I move toward the front door. "Overnight?"

"I'll be back first thing in the morning."

"I don't know, Son."

"And you can give me something off your list."

"I think Della's planning to bake a cake… or something."

"It's already been three days." A weight drops from my chest all the way down to my feet.

Dad stares at me, pitiful, quizzical.

"Alright," I say. "I'll call."

Jonathan is waiting on the steps. "What took you so long?" He stands and sees my dad. "Oh, hey Dr. Williamson."

Dad reaches out and claps Jonathan on the shoulder. "Sorry you couldn't make the trip."

"Believe me," Jonathan says, rubbing his arm. "I wanted to be in Florida."

I'm shivering. It's too cold to just stand around in the yard.

"You're all moved in?"

"Yes, Sir. Mom and Dad are still cleaning. Brian drove back to school this morning. My truck is loaded with the last stuff from the garage."

"Speaking of which…" I'm stepping onto the sidewalk. "We should go. I'll call later, Dad."

"Alright." Dad waves and stands there a moment.

We walk down the driveway, and when we get to the truck, I can finally breathe. "Let's get the fuck out of here."

The house Jonathan's parents bought is south of town, down a gravel road that isn't far from a two-lane paved highway. There is a sunny patch large enough for Jonathan's mother's garden, but the rest of the land is densely wooded oak-hickory forest. It's the kind of forest my mother loved. Jonathan eases the truck into the driveway, two ruts of glistening red mud that will harden to permanent ridges once the spring rains are over. He makes a three-point turn to back up to the garage. "We can save unloading for later," he says, pulling the key from the ignition and pressing down the emergency brake with his foot.

The walkway is flagstone grown over with last year's weeds. Chrysanthemum skeletons huddle near the foundation on either side of the door. "My mom hates the front. The first thing she said she wants to do is build a porch." He turns the house key inside the deadbolt. "Or, should I say, she wants me and Dad and Brian to build a porch." The door gives way with a nudge from his shoulder and opens onto a bright, stone-tiled entrance, windows sweeping from the floor to the open second-story ceiling. The familiar matching blue sofa and recliner slump together in the middle of the living room, laden with cardboard boxes and surrounded by stacks of more boxes set randomly on the floor. The kitchen is connected to the living room, resuming the stone tiles from the entryway and continuing the pattern to a set of French doors that opens to a deck.

"Come see." Jonathan leads me to a view of the forest that spreads out from the double doors. Trees grow just beyond the deck.

"This is excellent." I lean against the railing next to Jonathan, looking out into the bare trees and the woods beyond. An ancient shagbark hickory waits in the stillness, its splayed bark sprung out like wings near the upper branches. There is a hint of green in the under story, cushioned by wet brown leaves. I rub my hands across my arms. There is no wind, but it is chilly.

"Let's get inside," Jonathan says.

Downstairs, at the bottom of the carpeted steps, Jonathan announces his domain. He brings me to the center of a large common room that opens to a second wooden deck, several other rooms and an area that looks like a bar.

I walk over to the liquor cabinet and check the shelves. I turn the knobs to test the sink on the backside of the bar. "Sweet."

"Wait 'til you see this." Jonathan opens a door near the stairs. It's his room. I recognize the dark wooden head and footboards stacked against the wall. A mattress covered with plaid sheets and matching maroon bedspread is on the floor near the middle of the room. "Don't mind the mess," Jonathan says, wading through to open the door on the far wall. It's a bathroom, though most of it is the shower. Ceramic tile and glass brick span the entire back wall, facing the same direction as the two decks. The garbled image of thousands of trees filters into the room.

"Holy shit." I run my hand along the tiled countertop and catch my image in the round mirror set between two circular windows. "I look like shit."

"Nothing a shower won't fix." Jonathan moves to the shower and reaches in. He turns both knobs, and I can see the water cascading beyond his profile. He pulls his shirt over his head, and I watch.

He unbuttons his pants and looks at me, smirking, and says, "Wait your turn."

I leave. Fucking flirt. I lie on his bed and think of the hair near his nipples, how it disappears until his navel, then trails in a thin black line to the patch surrounding his cock.

It's like this: I see him step into the shower with his back to the nozzle and imagine the water pour over his head.

For as intensely awkward and embarrassed as I felt around Matt, I am fluid and confident with Jonathan. I unzip my sweatshirt, slide out of my pants and tee shirt and throw all of my clothes on the floor in a pile near Jonathan's. I step within the ceramic and glass enclosure, opposite my friend, whose eyes are closed beneath the bubbles migrating from the top of his head to his chin. Leaning against the cold tile, I watch through the steam, enjoying the sensation of heat and chill and the beginning of an erection.

"I learned a new trick while you were gone," Jonathan says. He takes a dark blue bottle from the built-in tile shelf and pours green shampoo onto his hand. "Stand over here," he motions to the glass brick wall on his left, "and face that way."

I move over and stand looking through the small patterned squares of glass.

"And put your hands up."

I lift my hands and fall forward, glad to follow instructions. Jonathan leans against me, pushing the top of his head into my upper back, forearms resting across my hips, and rubbing the thick liquid between both hands. Tree branches shimmer in front of me, the glass and mortar hold my weight, and the water from the shower splashes across my calves and ankles. Jonathan's hands reach for me, gliding a mixture of ice and heat slowly up and down. I arch my back and Jonathan keeps himself curved behind me, hugging me hard and squeezing his arms tighter around my waist. In a shudder that spans the entire length of my body, I come onto the tile floor between my feet.

I wish.

I shower alone after Jonathan leaves to unload his truck. I stare at the trees shimmering through the glass brick as the water pulses across my shoulders. A week is a long time to be away. Jonathan knows I want him, but he always says no, we're too close for that, I'm too young, he doesn't want to corrupt me.

He wants to be with someone, but not me, and I don't know why.

But who am I to be jealous? I had my time with Matt, right?

CHAPTER THREE

A rainbow flag hangs just inside the street front window. The door is held open by a huge white guy dressed in a torn black T-shirt and a striped knit cap. He clicks the stud on his tongue against his front teeth and nods at me and Jonathan, waving us into the throbbing smoke of the only gay bar in town.

"That guy is fucking large!" I yell into Jonathan's ear. We stand in the line fanning out from the register, just inside the door.

"Don't let him find you in the bathroom," Jonathan says.

At the register, a tall person of indeterminate gender tells us it's ten bucks. His hand is wide enough to palm a regulation basketball, his long fingers ending in manicured nails. We hand over the money.

We walk in, and I stare. Tall stringy boys in black lounge alongside handfuls of women looking tough in wife-beater tees and spiky hair. The dance area is raised two feet off the floor and is nothing more than plywood on painted two-by-fours. Tables hug the edges, and heads are turned, enjoying the show. Older women laugh and point at dancers. Middle-aged men stand alone or in pairs, mesmerized by the stage. Among the smoke and gyrating bodies, two thin blonde teens, not much older than Jonathan and I, curl into each other. They wear tight jeans and even tighter shirts, and they face the crowd, one in front of the other, ass to crotch.

"Let's get a drink." Jonathan tugs at my elbow.

Neat rows of bottled liquor line the glass shelves behind the bartender. "How are we going to do that?"

Jonathan looks around, surveying the onlookers. "Stay with me."

"Right," I say, and I follow him, turning sideways to slide through bodies that won't move out of the way. I can't help but rub against a guy with a tight, flowery, button-down shirt. But my ass doesn't even get grabbed once.

When we stop, it's on a patio that connects two separate areas, one with the dance floor we just passed, the other with video games placed randomly against the walls. We scan the crowd.

"Check out that guy," Jonathan says, looking back toward the edge of the bar.

I turn slightly and see that it's the guy with the flower-printed shirt. He has a bottle in his hand and is watching the dance floor. Two men approach him. They are well dressed. All three of them are probably twenty-something. "The guy in the flowers?"

"Yeah. What do you think?"

"Cute, but he's with those other guys."

"Nah," said Jonathan. "He's alone. They're just saying hello."

The two men drift away. The one in the flower print takes a drink from his bottle and turns to look in our direction, smiles, and then goes back to watching the dance floor. A woman with short, spiky hair walks up to him then, an older woman. I keep watching her. She looks my direction. "Shit!" I lean into Jonathan. "That's my first grade teacher!"

"No way." He studies her. "Say hi to her."

"I can't."

"Theo." Jonathan punches me in the ribs. "If she's in here, she's probably lesbian. She's not going to care if you're gay. She'll introduce us to that guy, and then he'll buy us a drink."

"Fuck." I push up my sleeves and walk slowly toward the bar. Jonathan presses from behind.

"Mrs. Sherman?" I touch her arm and she turns.

"Yes?" She finishes a swallow of beer. "It's been awhile since anyone's called me *that*."

"Umm, I'm Theo Williamson…first grade, Rountree Elementary." I hold out my hand.

Mrs. Sherman takes my hand in hers, and her fingers are warm and smooth. "Oh, Theo, you always had such good manners."

"You remember?"

Smile lines curve out from her eyes, and she says of course, and she introduces me to Tom, the guy in the flower-print shirt. I push Jonathan, maybe a little too hard, toward Tom, and they shake hands. Tom offers to buy us all drinks and Jonathan offers to wait at the bar with him. I'm not sure I want to walk away. But I do. Mrs. Sherman and I go together toward the patio to find a table, away from the loud techno blasting from the wall of speakers. Her hair isn't blonde anymore, but platinum and gray and she probably spends more money to have it styled than I could make in a month of mowing lawns. Maybe she doesn't teach first grade anymore.

"You can call me Carol," she says when we sit down together at the table.

"That's too weird."

"No weirder than meeting up here," she says, and she raises her bottle to me in a salute.

I agree. I watch the crowd with her for a few minutes.

"So, what brings you here, Theo?"

I clear my throat. "I guess the same reason most folks are here." I stare at the people walking past, and then turn to look at her. "Why are you here?"

She smiles. "It's not just gay folks who show up at a place like this. There are some straight people too."

"You're straight?"

"Yeah," she says and takes a drink and another drag on her cigarette. "And I enjoy watching men with men." She leans forward and pats my knee. "Hope I'm not embarrassing you too much." She relaxes in her chair, the end of her cigarette glowing bright with a long inhalation. "But really," she blows the smoke over my head, "I enjoy anything masculine when it comes to sex. Almost like being a woman is just incidental to who I am."

I nod and look away.

"I come here with Tom sometimes. He's my boss."

"You still teach?"

"I stopped teaching a few years ago, after my husband died." She taps her cigarette over the black melamine ashtray. "I decided it was time for a change." She stares through the open doorway, watching the dance floor. "You know, I lost my son too."

"Oh," I say.

"He would be as old as Tom. I guess that's why I'm so sweet on the guy. Not to mention how cute he is."

"Right," I say, and I politely excuse myself to the bathroom. If I didn't really have to go, I would head to the bar for Jonathan. Instead, I am jostled along between bodies in the other direction until I can find the door marked "Men." Underneath, scratched into the wood is written "Lovely Ladies" and "Boys, Too." I push the door open to the smell of old piss and sweat. Two people are kissing near the sink. They are both black, and one is obviously male. He looks like a gymnast, his dark bare shoulders, back, and waist ending abruptly in a belt and blue jeans. Seated on the counter is a thin, light chocolate-colored, mostly female person dressed in matching striped pants and shirt. Part of her ass is showing, revealing a waist no thicker than the top of my leg. I use the urinal farthest away from them and concentrate on the stream splashing over the stained porcelain, trying not to hear their moaning, sucking noises.

When I get back out to the patio, Mrs. Sherman is alone at the table, two beers set in front of her. "Tom left this for you," she says, pushing the bottle toward me.

"Where'd he go?"

"I think they wanted to dance," she says, lighting a cigarette with a shiny metal lighter. She inhales and then sits back with her beer resting on the arm of her chair. "They're certainly enjoying themselves."

I lean forward to see the view from Carol's angle. Jonathan and Tom are dancing near one corner of the raised floor. Jonathan is facing the crowd and Tom is behind him, both hands on Jonathan's waist.

"Want to join them?"

"Finish your drink first?"

"Oh, I didn't mean with me," she laughs. "You go on up there and dance. I'll save our table."

I take a long drink of my beer and push my chair back. "Are you sure?"

"No, go ahead. I'll have more fun watching."

I walk around to the far side of the dance floor to find the steps, passing a tower of speakers tall enough to belt out sound for a rock concert. The music thumps and pulses through my chest, matching the strobe lights and fog. I feel pushed and pulled by sound and light and bodies in motion. Jonathan and Tom are in the middle of a crowd, facing each other, but they move apart so I can join them. Jonathan turns toward me and leans into my shoulder. "Let's take him home."

"Get his number," I yell. Jonathan nods and turns around, backing his ass into my crotch. I put my hands on Jonathan's waist. Tom stands in front of both of us. We dance sandwiched. Jonathan spins around, and then moves to the side so Tom and I are facing each other. Tom approaches, matching his hips to mine. He makes his way around me, and then dances behind me, running his hands slowly from my lats down to my thighs. I go with it. He smells good, and his hands never hesitate. I lean into him, pressing back with my ass until we are touching all the way from thighs to shoulders. Jonathan is dancing with someone else.

"You've never been here before?"

I shake my head.

"How did you meet Jonathan?" His mouth is just under my ear. He runs his nose along my neck.

"Neighbors."

"Same dorm?"

I turn to face him. I pull him close and speak into his ear. "High school."

"Shit."

"Did he tell you we were older?"

"No," Tom says, pressing his mouth to my ear. We switch places as we talk back and forth. "Just a guess. Are you guys legal?"

"To drink?"

Tom pushes me away, smiling. He pulls me in close again. "No," he says. He draws me in by the waist and doesn't say any more. When the music fades into drum machine thumping, Tom signals toward the table where Carol is sitting. "I need a break."

I nod and see Jonathan surrounded by three or four wispy guys. They look like the blondes from earlier in the evening.

When Jonathan sees me, he raises his arms and breaks away from the group, meeting me halfway. "Where's Tom?"

"At the table."

"What do you think?"

"Nice, but he's too old. He thinks we're in college."

"That's alright."

"I told him we're in high school."

"You dork."

"Sorry." I shrug.

When we get back to the table, Carol and Tom are talking, and there are four fresh beers. "Here," Tom says, holding up two of the bottles. "Drink up before we're discovered. I hear there's a birthday boy in our midst."

We all raise our bottles and they say cheers, and I drink a very long drink.

The patio is quieter than the dance floor. We are close enough to see the dancers and feel the bass vibrating through the wooden decking, but far enough away that we can all hear each other without screaming. Jonathan sits next to Tom and I sit next to Carol. "Thanks," I say to Tom, not quite leaning back in my seat. "But we probably shouldn't have accepted the drinks."

"Come on, it's your birthday," Tom says. "And besides, I did the same thing before I could buy my own."

"Well, I didn't," Carol says. She winks at me. "But I don't mind contributing to the delinquency of minors every once in a while." She takes a long drag off her cigarette. "Don't go doing anything too crazy just because it's your birthday." Smoke drifts from her in a slow arc. Tom lights a cigarette too, nodding and relaxing into his seat. Jonathan looks happy.

"So, how's your dad these days, Theo?" Carol asks. "Still teaching?"

"Umm," I start. My mom died when I was in first grade, so Mrs. Sherman knows what that year was like. I take a breath and say that I have a step-mom now and she teaches junior high math, and my dad is still in the Math Department at Missouri State.

She rests her hand on my arm. She reminds me of that field trip that my mom helped with, and I see a glimpse of a family that I've almost forgotten. Carol pauses, takes a drink of beer and another hit from her cigarette. "Your dad read a Christmas story to our class."

I forgot. That year is a blur that I don't think about much. I tell Carol about the car accident, and when she asks if my dad was hurt badly, I give her a list of my dad's injuries, telling her how both of his knees and ankles were shattered, his collarbone and several ribs were broken, and his cheekbone and skull fractured. I don't say anything about the way my dad's glasses have carved a permanent scar into his face, or how the doctors have re-broken both his knees to loosen the calcified deposits behind his kneecaps.

"His skull?" Carol repeats.

"Yeah," I say, looking away. "Traumatic brain injury. He was in a coma for a week."

"But he's better now?"

"Um-hmm." I haven't tried to describe what my dad is like since the accident to anyone in a long time. "He's better, but he's not the same."

Tom and Jonathan are watching the stage, both quiet and listening. I can't see the dancers, but I don't want to turn away from Carol.

"I'm so sorry," she says, touching my knee.

"It's okay," I say. "It's not so bad anymore." Which is mostly true.

She crushes the end of her cigarette under her shoe, a red, leather flat, and sits back. "Oh, I remember what I wanted to ask you," she says. "Do you remember Michael Ashbury?"

"Sure," I say. I'm hoping she isn't going to tell me that Michael is dead.

"I saw him a few months ago. He said he goes to some meeting once a week for gay and lesbian youth. Know anything about it?"

"Is it like AA for queers?"

She laughs. "I don't think so. It didn't sound like they were trying to cure anyone." She turns to Tom. "What's that group they have for gay youth?"

"Hmm." He leans forward for his beer. "I think it's called Youth Out or something. I'm not so sure I'd send anyone to it. I heard one of the adult facilitators, some med student intern, was scamming on the younger boys, kids in junior high."

"Scamming young boys, eh?" Carol's eyebrows are raised. "That's not good."

Tom empties his beer and sits back.

My head feels heavy. The music is pulsing just below my heartbeat and I keep thinking I'll say something I'll regret.

"Pardon me," Tom says and pushes his chair back to leave for the men's room.

"He's a good guy." Carol says when he leaves. "Just coming off a relationship."

Jonathan turns in his chair to watch Tom walk away. Jonathan fidgets with his beer, then pushes his chair away after saying he'll be back.

I nod. "Maybe we should go soon."

"Soon," Jonathan says and then heads to the bathroom.

Carol is saying something. She leans closer. "Don't worry about him." She is looking at Jonathan. "Tom is a sweetheart. Just a little lonelier than is good for him." I'm only getting part of it, like she's been talking a long time. "I used to worry," she says, "but when I lost my husband, and then my son, something in me said *relax*. I realized there wasn't much about the world I could change, except myself."

I set my bottle on the table. I'm trying to keep the thread of her voice.

"You've been through a lot, Theo, but I think you're going to be okay. I think Jonathan's going to be okay too. He seems like a smart boy. I've seen so many kids hurting because nobody understands them, and because life seems to be dishing out more than they can handle." She lights another cigarette. I've lost count. "It's hard to give up thinking you can change anyone but yourself, because it feels like you're giving up. But when you do that," here she points at some *that* in the air with her cigarette, "is actually when you find how strong you are." She looks at me and laughs. "I've gone and started preaching." She squeezes my thigh and then relaxes into her chair. "You're a sweet one, Theo, and you'll make it just fine."

I take a breath. It's the beer. Della sometimes does this after too many gin and tonics.

Jonathan and Tom are talking and laughing at something. I want to be in on it, but I'm too tired to pull it off without looking jealous. I watch Jonathan's hands describing something in the air to Tom, long fingers forming shapes, and then combing through that glossy black hair. I'm staring at Jonathan's pockets, at the outline of the fists now shoved casually inside.

"Hey, are you alright?" Jonathan is standing on the other side of the table.

"Yeah."

"Want to call it a night?" Tom asks.

Carol puts out her cigarette in the ashtray. "Sounds good to me." She stands next to Tom and Jonathan. They are waiting.

I stand. The music is pounding my head.

On the sidewalk out front, Tom offers us each a bottle of water. "Drink some of this to clear the cobwebs," he says to me.

I drink it in one long sip.

We walk to the parking lot, coming to Carol's car first. "You're driving?" Tom asks.

"Yep." She flashes the keys and unlocks the passenger door for Tom, then goes around to the other side. "Oh, take care, boys." She comes back and gives Jonathan a hug, and then me. "Happy birthday, Hon."

Tom looks at us both. "G'night, Theo." He holds me in a full embrace. "And happy birthday."

"Thanks," I say into his shoulder.

Tom grabs Jonathan and kisses him. I look away, trying to remember where Jonathan parked the truck.

You alright there, Big Boy?"

"Yeah," I say, buckling my seatbelt.

"That bathroom was nasty," Jonathan says. "If I hadn't been so damn horny, I would have told him to wait until we could find something cleaner."

"But you didn't."

"Nah." He puts the truck into gear and starts driving.

"How did he rate?"

"Hmm." Jonathan taps his fingers on the steering wheel. "An eight."

"I've been replaced."

Jonathan thumps my leg. "Hey," he says. "That's not what we're about."

"No," I say. I watch out the window as the streetlights give way to the darker highway.

"What's this? You get to come home and tell me about some guy you blow?" His voice is too loud for the little cab.

"I'm just tired." I lean my head against the glass behind the bench seat. "It's just shit."

Jonathan is quiet for a few minutes. "Theo, you know I meet guys."

"I know."

"What gives?"

It takes a while to speak. "I've never seen you with someone else." I've been putting myself into the stories Jonathan tells me about meeting guys at the park. At the library. The cold marble partitions in the bathroom stall at the old public library pressed against my own back, my hands on some guy's head, pressing a face to my crotch until he comes and not letting go until every last drop is swallowed. Or, it's Jonathan standing above me, trying not to moan but unable to keep his voice from bouncing around the marble enclosure, up from the tiny black and white octagonal ceramic floor tiles and all the way to the twenty-foot high ceilings left over from some other distant time.

We turn into Jonathan's driveway and sit in the truck in darkness. Jonathan turns to face me, but he doesn't say anything.

I roll my head across the back window, so my body is facing forward but my head is tilted, turned toward Jonathan. "What?"

"I think that vacation fucked you up."

"No shit."

"Maybe we should have gotten a video tonight or something. I didn't mean to weird you out. I just wanted you to have a little fun for your birthday."

"It was fun. I'll get over it. I just need some sleep."

He leads me to the back of the house, along a gravel path lined with landscape timbers. A sodium light buzzes overhead. It's mounted on a tree, and Jonathan shoots at it with his fingers as we pass. I stare up at the light through the outline of branches and clinging oak leaves. My head is muddy.

Jonathan unlocks the back door and closes it quietly behind us. His parents don't wait up for him, an advantage of staying here instead of at my house. When I come out of the bathroom, Jonathan is unrolling a sleeping bag. "This alright?"

"Yep." I unbutton my shirt. I go down on the floor and crawl across to the sleeping bag. My head sinks into a pillow.

The overhead light is off, but a bulb from the bathroom glows behind Jonathan. He is taking off his clothes in the doorway, a dark silhouette.

Later, when he is asleep, I lie awake, looking at him. His mattress is six inches higher than the floor. I reach up and touch the sheet near his face and watch him breathe. His hair falls across his brow. I lean up and kiss the outside of his rolled up fist, and then I am asleep.

CHAPTER FOUR

Rain has stained the trees dark. I'm running in a pair of Jonathan's shorts and a smoky shirt from last night. Wet leaves blanket the ground beneath the trunks of gnarled oaks lining the raised edges of the gravel road. The roadbed has sunk lower than the forest floor from years of erosion. Further into the woods, a hint of green, so slight it seems like a haze, shimmers beneath the hickory and sassafras and leggy saplings gliding by on either side. A damp silence surrounds the one-lane road that leads to Jonathan's new house. I am lulled into a quiet thankfulness for the morning and for being in Missouri again with Jonathan.

Yet, I am also convinced he is an asshole. Yes, Tom is attractive. But a blowjob in the bathroom?

At the house, Jonathan is helping his mom make breakfast.

"Morning, Mrs. Norton."

"Oh, hi Theo." Her hands shake as she flips the bacon. Veins show through her thin skin—she is old. She started late having kids, and now she looks more like a grandmother. "Welcome to our mansion," she says, and she takes a long drag on a cigarette.

"I love it," I say. "The woods are gorgeous."

"Dr. Norton promised me we'd move out to the woods before we got too old." She turns her head away from the stove and coughs. "Bastard made me wait long enough."

Jonathan stirs the pot of hissing potatoes and rolls his eyes. "Watch the language."

"Yes, Dear," she says. They only joke like this when Dr. Norton is out of the room.

Jonathan looks at me but I ignore him. I ask Mrs. Norton if she wants me to set the table.

"So charming, Theo." She inhales and then blows smoke out the window over the kitchen sink. "Let's use the good plates," she says. She hands them to me, and I arrange them along with the silverware and napkins and glasses on the table like my mom taught me.

At breakfast, Dr. Norton does most of the talking. "Yep, we had to miss Florida this year," he says. "We had to miss it." Mrs. Norton and Jonathan and I chew in silence. Nobody argues with Dr. Norton. He sniffs the air. "Sheila, have you been smoking again?"

"Of course not, darling," she says and coughs a little, and then she keeps eating.

Jonathan's face has a hard look to it, like he's on the verge of saying something. I wish he would.

"Why are we using the good China?" Dr. Norton asks.

"Why not?" Jonathan says.

"It was my idea." Mrs. Norton intervenes. "Our first big breakfast in the new house."

"Good thing they didn't break." Dr. Norton pushes egg yolk around on his plate with his toast. "Got any plans today, Son?"

"Homework," Jonathan says, and he keeps eating, his eyes downcast. The rest of the meal is quiet, and then later, Jonathan drives me home. "Don't be thinking you can keep those," he says. "That's my favorite pair of jeans."

The denim of Jonathan's pants is stretched tight across my thighs. "Maybe you shouldn't have been so quick to lend them," I say. My canvas bag is at my feet on the floorboard, reeking of smoky, sweaty clothes. I shift to pull the fabric away from my crotch. "You're too skinny."

"It's my rigorous workout schedule." Jonathan turns the corner onto my street.

"What workout?"

"You know, keeping the men happy burns lots of calories."

"Just how many men are you keeping happy?"

Jonathan pulls into my driveway and puts the truck in neutral. "Hmm. Let's see, I think I got to six last week."

"What?"

Jonathan laughs. "Joking." He smiles wickedly.

"Straight up. What did you do while I was gone?"

He punches my shoulder. "I helped my folks move. Remember? I was too fucking tired to go cruising."

"Glad to hear."

"Lighten up. I'm dishing you shit." He rests his hand on the gearshift. "I've got something for you." He pulls out a paper bag from beneath his seat.

"More liquor?"

"Maybe." He sets the package on my lap and waits while I open it. Inside is a weathered wooden frame. Behind the glass is a black and white photo of the two of us on a merry-go-round. Our profiles are sharp against a background of blurred trees and grass. The camera was on a timer, a 35mm he borrowed from his brother for a photography class at school. I'm holding onto a bar and pushing against the ground with one foot. Jonathan jumps on and then we both scramble toward the middle. The merry-go-round is tilted, so we slide with each revolution. The photo catches us just before Jonathan falls into me, laughing too hard to hold on.

It's a moment I forgot, the mess of colliding to the ground, out of control.

"What, do you hate it?"

"I love it," I say. I fold it back into the bag and wish we weren't already parked in front of my house. I want to hold him. I want to tell him that I want to hold him. "Thanks," I say. "I've got to go."

"Let's take a trip next weekend," Jonathan says. "Camp out."

"I've got a meet Saturday."

"Basketball game Tuesday night?"

"Alright," I say. We tap knuckles and I get out of the truck and watch Jonathan drive away. Several black plastic bags of trash line the street at the edge of his old yard. The driveway lies empty and the curtained windows are closed.

Della and my dad are both sitting at the dining room table reading different sections of the Sunday paper. "I expected a call from you, Theo," Della says as she stands from her chair. She refills her coffee and leans against the counter stirring in cream and sugar.

"I'm sorry." I scratch my head. "I forgot."

"Please don't let it happen again."

My dad stands and stretches his back and asks if I'm hungry. "We got bagels." He opens the paper bag on the table and looks inside, then holds the bag to his nose. "Two sesame and one cinnamon." He looks up at me.

"Mrs. Norton made us breakfast."

"How's the new place?" Della asks.

My dad sits again, slowly, and Della rejoins him at the table.

"It's nice. Lots of windows. Trees."

"They're out in the woods," Dad says. "I feel bad for not helping."

"You shouldn't be helping anyone move with those knees of yours. This is the first time they've missed the camping trip." Della looks over at me. "Speaking of which. You have some work to do."

"I know," I mumble to the counter. I lean forward and rest my elbows on the tile, my forehead in my hands. "I'll do it this afternoon."

"Your father and I are going to a movie, so we'll need the van, that is, if it's still rnning."

"What's wrong with it?"

"The engine light kept coming on last night. We probably pushed it too far driving all the way from Florida in one day."

My dad puts the paper down. "Cars are meant to go all day."

"Then what is it?" Della shifts forward and puts her chin on her palm, ready to hear his diagnosis.

"I don't know. An oil change? How long's it been?"

"Two months. I keep track of our car quite well, thank you, and everything else in this household." She looks down at the table. I think I'm supposed to feel sorry for her, but I'm too tired.

"Thank you, Dear," Dad says and reaches across to set his hand on her leg.

"Anyway," she says to me, "you need to take care of the sleeping bags this morning and your dad has to go to the hardware store, so you two can go together—without me—now that you and your father can drive."

"When did that happen?"

"Your dad drove yesterday and did just fine." She looks at him and then at me. "Here are the keys." She sets them on the table and leaves with her coffee.

Shit. I go away for a night and now my dad can drive again.

My dad and I are stuffing sleeping bags into the trunk. "Where's Samantha?" I ask.

"She went to church with Kate this morning."

"Great. Just what I need—a sister who knows the gospel."

"That wouldn't be so bad."

"When's the last time you saw a Christian preaching love for gays?"

Dad stands there. He remembers, doesn't he?

"Can I drive?"

"Sure, Kid." He reaches in his coat pocket and pulls out the keys. He holds them a second, thinking, and then tosses them. "When are you taking that driving test?"

"Whenever I get in enough practice hours." I take the keys and start the car. "Maybe you could give me a ride to school in the morning—I could drive."

"Della's leaving early to bring the van to the shop. She'd probably make *me* walk to campus if she thought my knees could take it."

I deflate.

"What about your bike?" he says.

"Yeah," I say. I used to ride to school with Jonathan. Now he doesn't live next door. I need to get my license, but I don't have a car. And now my dad is trying to solve my problems.

My parents offered to let me use the truck when I got my license, back when there was a truck. Della took me to see it one day.

It was like this: She and I were arguing in the van while Dad was at physical therapy. The truck could be fixed. I was sure of it. When we got to the junkyard north of Springfield, she wouldn't leave the van. I went by myself to the corrugated trailer marked "Office" and asked an old guy with a stutter and grease beneath his nails if he knew where the truck might be. He was quiet when he stopped at the end of one of the rows in the back, near a bunch of piles that looked more like metal for recycling than like vehicles. The old guy pointed to a pile, and then I recognized the dark green paint of my dad's little truck. The metal parts were all smashed together, the dashboard nearly touching the back of the mangled bench seat except for a few inches of space by the steering column. Near the driver's side door were gouges that looked like claw marks, as if the paramedics saved my dad from a huge grizzly bear attack instead of just a car accident.

The laundromat is mostly empty. After setting the sleeping bags next to the washers, I walk out to the car with Dad to get my backpack.

A blue hatchback has pulled up next to our van. A man steps out and then leans in to grab a basket off the front seat. He has on a cap, so I don't see his face until he stands to close the car door. It's Matt. His eyes lock with mine, and a wave of something crosses his face before he is able to say anything.

My dad speaks first. "Hey there. I see you made it home safely."

"Hey, David. Yeah. I got in last night." He hesitates. "Hey, Theo."

"Hey," I say. I turn away to open the back door and reach for my backpack.

Matt lifts his basket of clothes. "They're renovating the washroom at my apartments."

"Theo's washing sleeping bags."

"I've got mine in the back," Matt says and nods toward his back seat.

"At least you'll have good company."

I'm standing on the sidewalk, waiting.

Matt's lips part to say something. He looks away from me. "I've got a stack of exams," he says to my dad. "I guess I left my grading to the last minute." He closes the front door with his hip and adjusts his cap.

"I'm going inside," I say. I look at my dad. "When will you be back?"

"An hour?"

"I'll be here." I start to let the door to the laundromat close, but Dad says to hold it open for Matt. I wait.

After an unmistakable look from me to Matt and back again, Dad says goodbye.

A knot pulls tight in my gut. Matt is balancing a basket loaded with clothes and stapled papers with one arm and an unrolled sleeping bag with the other. I watch my dad drive across the parking lot with my back against the glass door. Matt brushes past me, his sleeping bag trailing behind.

The door closes silently and I push aside a wheeled skeleton cart. I put each sleeping bag in a separate washer and load them with quarters and detergent. Matt is on the other side of a double row of washers filling two top-loading machines with shirts and jeans and socks. He faces away from me. His hair tumbles out of the back of his cap and catches on his collar, shifting each time he lifts his arms with more pieces of clothing. He is wearing a checkered button-down shirt, probably with a T-shirt underneath. He would look good no matter what he was wearing.

He turns, but I don't look away in time. I tap the top of the washer. He is beautiful and I like him and I hate him.

Matt puts his hands in his pockets. I look away, and then I take a deep breath. I get my backpack. The present from Jonathan is still in the bottom of my bag. I grab the novel and try to read. And I try not to look up when Matt leaves to get something else from his car.

I stare at the typed words in my hands. Cold air brushes my ankles and the wall vibrates with the closing of the heavy glass door. Matt's footsteps aren't audible, but I keep my head down and listen, trying to follow him walking back to the washers and gathering his papers, and then sitting with his work in his lap.

"Theo."

He is standing right fucking across from me, leaning against a washer. He sits in a chair two seats away.

I lay down my book.

"Theo, I want to apologize."

I let out my breath. "Don't."

He holds his students' papers in clenched hands. "What happened was completely my fault."

I don't say anything.

He crosses one leg over the other. He sets the papers on the chair next to him and turns to me. "I feel really bad about what I said to you. About what happened. I didn't handle it well. I don't want you to think you did anything wrong." He stops.

My ears are pulsing. I keep running my thumbnail along the edge of my book. Why does he have to be so perfect?

"If you feel like you need to talk to someone about it, I'll understand." Matt has practiced these words.

"What?" I stare at him.

"It shouldn't be a secret you've got to keep."

"From who?"

"Your parents."

"God, I would never tell my parents. They'd kill me."

"No, they'd be mad at me, and that's not your problem. It's mine."

I look away. "I'm not going to tell my parents."

Matt sits there, the papers open in his lap. "Don't let this blow you off course," he says after a long silence. "Most adults won't tell you, but we're fucked up, too." He gathers his papers. "I've gotta get some work done," he says, and he moves to a chair in another row, far away.

Outside, it is cold and quiet. No back-and-forth wash cycles. No absence of air to breathe. The laundromat is on the fringe of a neighborhood of two-story houses chopped into apartments for students from campus. I walk, concentrating on the cracks and the brown grass runners tangled along the edges of the pavement. Beer cans are scattered between the sidewalk and the street. No way am I going to this school when I graduate from high school. The further away, the better.

I shove my hands deeper into my pockets and turn back. The fucking sleeping bags have to go in the dryers. I'm not going to notice the other side of the laundromat.

There are more cars parked out front and more people inside shoving clothes and shit into washers. Matt is gone. The sleeping bags are on spin, so I sit and watch. A college girl in pajama bottoms and a ribbed tank top sits tailor-style on the folding table near me. She is hunched over a magazine. It's too cold to be dressed in so little. She's pretty, but I don't care. Seeing the skin on her arms and the ring through her nose does nothing for me.

Samantha is in the living room with Della, playing a board game on the coffee table. "Hey, Theo. Want to play the next round?"

"Nah," I say. "I've got homework."

"Please, please."

Della finishes her turn and is watching, but doesn't say anything. It isn't like her to keep quiet when she could be taking up for Samantha.

"Sorry, Sis."

"What do you want us to do with these, Dear?" Dad is standing in the foyer with the bags draped across his arms.

"Are they dry?"

"I think so."

Della gets up from the floor. "Here, let me see." She runs her hand inside each. "Nope. Theo, why don't you take these from your dad? Turn them inside out and hang them on the line in the basement." She tells him he shouldn't be carrying four sleeping bags by himself, and would I please take off my shoes and leave them by the door when I'm done.

Yes, I should have grabbed the bags myself.

After my chore in the basement, I close myself in my room. A Rufus Wainwright CD is in my disc player. I put on my headphones and lean against the wall, listening to song after song and staring through the blinds. I finally relax when my favorite song, the one about being with one guy, starts playing. It is one of the few songs where Rufus plays guitar instead of piano, and I listen to the words, surprised that such a party boy would ever want to be with only one person.

Two summers ago, soon after the Big Talk with Dad and Della, my dad and I went to a concert in Kansas City without telling Della. He said we were going to see the Chiefs when he gave me the tickets for my fourteenth birthday. We went to the game, but the next night, we saw Rufus in concert. Young, beautiful, and definitely gay.

Jonathan and I wanted to see Rufus in St. Louis last summer, but we couldn't figure out how to pull it off. My parents don't know Jonathan is gay. They can't. It's dangerous enough in this fundamentalist town that I like guys, that my parents know about it, but so far, they've never discussed it with anyone outside the family. Even Dad, with his scrambled brain, keeps it to himself. Or maybe he's just forgotten. But if my parents knew about Jonathan, they might tell his parents, and then he would be dead. That's how it is. Jonathan says his parents can never find out about either of us. He says his dad laughed when Matthew Shepard was killed. *Righteous retribution* he called it. His dad is educated enough to teach at a college, but he's a Missouri conservative, and according to Jonathan, there's no amount of schooling that can fix that.

There is a knock at my door. It's Della. She sits on the edge of my bed and waits for me to take off my headphones.

"Can we talk?"

"About what?"

She closes the door and then settles further onto the bed, turned semi-sideways so she isn't quite facing away. "Your father is getting better every day."

"Yeah." Great. I do *not* need a lecture. "Is this about the sleeping bags? I'm sorry, okay?"

"Part of it is… but part of it's not. I've been letting things slide with you and Samantha. Your dad needed so much care at first that I lost track of everything else." She pauses. "I guess I'm still distracted," she says. "I'm so sorry about your birthday."

"It doesn't matter."

"We wanted to celebrate with you last night." She curls the edge of the bedspread in her fingertips, and then goes on about how I should have called. "Anyway, I'm going to make teriyaki steak and rice tonight."

She knows that's my favorite.

"But, we need to talk about some things…"

I look away. I want to put on my headphones, but I don't.

"Your dad's cognitive awareness has gotten better, and he's been noticing some things that I should have noticed on my own."

"What things?"

"Well, you were anxious during the trip to Florida. And your dad said you seemed very uncomfortable this morning at the laundromat." She smoothes the bedspread near her leg and plows ahead, making up for the last eleven months. "He and I have been wondering if something is bothering you. Something other than us forgetting your birthday."

I wish she would just keep letting things slide. "No," I say.

"I think we need to talk about *physical* relationship things."

"I don't have any *physical* relationship things to talk about."

"Theo, I made some calls today—"

Oh god.

"Let me finish," she says.

I pull my knees to my chest and hold my legs.

"Before the accident, any time your father or I tried to bring up the subject of homosexuality, you said that you could handle relationship stuff on your own." She waits, biting her lower lip, but I don't say anything. "I called Jonathan's parents this morning to see what time you might be coming home. You'd already left, but when I asked if you boys had fun last night, Mrs. Norton said she'd noticed that Jonathan's clothes smelled smoky and she didn't know where you two could have gone that was so smoky."

I still don't say anything. I don't want to think because even that might be too loud.

"Would you like to tell me where you were?"

"We just drove around mostly."

She takes my hand and holds it so that I can see the back. The stamp from the bar still stains my skin.

"I know there are only two bars in town that let in anyone under 21. Which one were you at?"

I look away.

"Theo, don't lie to me."

I don't answer.

"Martha's Vineyard?"

I rock back and forth. "Yes."

"So, now I'm wondering why you and *Jonathan* would go to a gay bar together."

Oh shit.

"Do Jonathan's parents know he's gay?"

"No," I say.

"And do they know that you are gay?"

"No," I say, my voice tight and small.

She takes a deep breath and sits straighter, looking away from me and at the slanted sunlight coming through the blinds. "You and Jonathan met when we moved into this house, right?"

"Yeah."

"How old were you? Twelve?"

"Eleven." I am sinking into my bed.

Della slides to the edge. Buying this house was the first big thing she and my dad did together after they got married. Della stares at her hands for a minute and then looks at me. "You, your father, and I need to have a serious talk." She stands to leave. "Tomorrow evening, I'll have Samantha go to a friend's house after dinner. I don't want you making any plans with Jonathan or going anywhere with him between now and then."

"Why?"

She turns the door handle. "This is one of those times that I expect you to honor my wishes. Understood?"

"Sure," I say. I'm already putting on my headphones She leaves and I close my eyes and push the play button again. What a fucking bummer. Every secret I've ever kept from them is about to get set out on the table and examined. I've got to talk with Jonathan during first hour. And I've got to make sure my bike is ready to ride for the morning. Joy.

CHAPTER FIVE

Fog has settled during the night, clinging to the streetlights and blanketing the houses and yards with grey. Gliding through upside-down cones of illuminated mist, I alternate putting one hand in my pocket and one hand on the handlebar. My fingers are frozen by the time I get to school.

Jonathan is waiting. "I called last night. What's up with Della?"

I slide open my lock and pull the metal door too hard. It slams against the next locker. "She's on to me, that's what."

"You mean the shit that happened in Florida?"

"Maybe." I lean into my locker, closer to Jonathan. "And you."

"Me?"

"Did your mom say anything to you yesterday?"

"She asked why my clothes smelled like smoke, but I told her we got a burger at the diner on State Street. It's always full of people smoking."

"Fuck." I close my locker.

We walk slowly to first hour. "I couldn't think of anything to say." Jonathan leans into me, avoiding passing shoulders and backpacks and elbows. "She saw the ink stain on my hand." I keep my voice low. "She asked if your parents know."

We round a corner and go into Mr. Burnett's classroom, Algebra II. Della and Dad expect me to love math because they love it. But I don't. I take a seat in the back, and Jonathan sits in the next desk over. The board is covered in Mr. Burnett's illegible chalk scratches. Most of the students aren't here yet, but he starts discussing the day's assignment anyway. It's as if spring break never happened. I lean forward and rest my head on my arm.

The rest of the morning is slow. First hour is the only class we have together, so I wait until lunch to see Jonathan again. We meet in the parking lot and walk to the truck together. An open campus is one of the few luxuries at Parkview High.

Jonathan gets in the truck and reaches across to unlock the passenger door. "Want to eat?"

I say sure. I sit in his truck and stare ahead with my backpack at my feet.

Jonathan drives awhile without saying anything. He pulls into a drive-up fast food place and orders the usual for both of us. "What do you think they'll do?"

"I don't know."

"How'd Della leave it last night?"

"She said we're having a *serious* talk tonight—me, her, and Dad." I'm black inside. I'm thinking of the fishermen in Florida who wade out each morning and cast nets across the waves. I'm caught in one of those weighted nets, pulled down into my seat, into a pit. I feel small and stupid trying to figure out how to protect Jonathan. "I don't want to think about it."

"Just say as little as possible," Jonathan says after the server comes. He starts eating, and he watches me squeeze ketchup onto a napkin on the dash.

"It's never that easy with her. She'll ask me shit outright, and it's got to be either a yes or no answer. I wish she'd just go back to worrying about Dad."

"Don't wish for that."

"He can drive now." I eat a bite of my burger. "He drove us to the laundromat." I dip my fries in the ketchup on the dash. I eat them three and four at a time. "Guess who was there? Matt. Fucking Matt. 'You don't have to keep it a secret,' he says."

"Asshole," Jonathan says. "He's taking advantage of you." He turns the key to light up the digital clock. "How old is he?"

"Late twenties."

"And he has kids?"

"Two. Girls."

"Does he know he's gay?"

"It was just one blow job."

"My point exactly. He's repressed." Jonathan rolls up his wrapper and throws his trash at my feet.

"Don't leave this shit in here." I grab the bag and shove it into Jonathan's lap. "Throw it at *your* feet if you don't want to throw it away."

He stares at me.

I thump the ugly pink-haired creature hanging from his rearview mirror. "When are you gonna get rid of this thing?"

"Lighten up, clean freak. I love my troll." He stops the naked plastic toy from swinging and rolls down the window to set the bags on the stainless steel platform. One of them rolls off as he backs out, but Jonathan drives away without stopping.

I watch the bag roll across the parking lot in the side-view mirror.

"How'd you get to school this morning?" he says.

"Bike."

"Want me to pick you up tomorrow?"

"No," I say.

"Call me tonight. I need to know if your parents are going to say something."

"What would you do?"

"I don't know," he says and breathes out a long, slow breath.

We never talk about Dr. Norton.

It was like this: We were in the front yard. Jonathan kicked the soccer ball to my right, and I stretched to reach it. I was fast, too fast, and the ball flew from my foot straight into the window we'd just washed. The shattering glass exploded into the living room. Dr. Norton ran out screaming. His arm was cut. "Son of a bitch!" he yelled at Jonathan, assuming he did it. He slapped Jonathan, shoved him to the ground. I stared at the bits of glass still falling away from the window frame. I wanted to wrestle Dr. Norton off Jonathan. But I didn't. I couldn't.

"Your parents are just freaked out," Jonathan says, "because they've been thinking all this time that you're a virgin." He's not taking this seriously. "Technically you are, but you could change that."

"Wrong."

Jonathan finds a parking space. "Matt might like it."

It's not Matt that I want to lose my virginity to.

"No," I say.

We leave the truck and split up just inside the front hallway. I go to chemistry and Jonathan goes to government.

"Stay strong," he says. He punches my arm.

"Yeah," I say. I head to class, to the eternity of afternoon that stretches out before me, wondering if the new kid Richard is the kind of guy Jonathan would lose his virginity to. If Jonathan is still a virgin.

I get to run in two hours, the only thing that might keep me from exploding.

This is the best and the worst part of the day. Being surrounded by naked guys is exquisitely painful. I've been practicing since junior high how to enjoy all that exposed skin without showing a visible response. Today, I'm agitated, so I don't notice the semi-nude bodies around me, not even Donovan, the most beautifully sculpted male in the entire school. He has dark brown hair and blue eyes, and after a day in the sun at a track meet, he'll have a dusting of freckles across his nose and his cheeks, and even his shoulders if he takes off his shirt. There is a scar just above his hip on the right side that I've always wanted to ask about.

At least two other guys on the team, Stevens and Steadman, are gay. I walked in on a kiss in the deserted locker room last fall, but I never said anything to them. They look like brothers, or cousins, maybe. Both have shaggy dirty blonde hair and tough, wiry bodies. Stevens is from one of the horse farms on the edge of town that has been swallowed up by car dealerships and new housing developments. Steadman lives in Boys Town. He lost his mom in a tornado and his dad is a crack head. Because Coach Eberhardt is friends with Della, I know more about members of the track team than I should.

I pull on my socks and tie my shoes and listen to Stevens and Steadman talk in low voices. They have each other, always stretching and warming up together, running as buddies. Best friends—that's how they look to everyone else.

And then there are guys that I *always* avoid—the shot and discus throwers, stocky Christian farm boys who make a point of using 'faggot' and 'queer' every other time they open their mouths. I have nothing in common with them, so it's easy to maintain distance and give just enough eye contact so they don't fuck with me. The runners who are too pansy or too tough get pushed around by farm boys looking to kick some ass. Safety is maintained by separateness, mediocrity.

Today I'm running behind Donovan, concentrating so hard on matching strides that I don't get to enjoy the view. We run four miles, from the high school to the edge of the university campus and back again. I'm tired and wishing Jonathan would be waiting at the parking lot to give me a ride. But he isn't.

I ride my bike and get home before anyone else. The microwave beeps. I look through the stack of mail. I pour the popcorn into a bowl, grab some pastries and a glass of milk and take it all to my room and start my homework.

The front door slams shut. "Theo?"

"Up here, Sam."

She pushes my door open and sits on the edge of my bed, breathing fast. Her face is flushed.

"Why so out of breath?"

"I ran home."

"From the bus stop at the end of the street?"

"No, I got off at Kate's house." She brushes her hair back from her face. "Don't tell Della and Dad, okay?"

"Who's gonna stop me?"

"I am, because I've got information that you really want."

"Yeah, right." When she doesn't say anything, I nudge her with my foot. "Spill it."

"Got any popcorn left?"

"Here." I hand her the bowl. "Now, gimme the goods."

"Well, last night, after you went to your room, I heard Della and Dad talking." She eats a few kernels of popcorn. "I heard your name several times, so I figured I'd get a little closer—you know how sometimes you can hear through the heater vents?"

"Yeah. So, what did you hear?"

She looks at me and takes a deep breath. "Theo, you know I'm not as innocent as you think I am."

"Innocent about what?"

"About sex and stuff like that."

"Who told you about sex?"

"Della of course told me the scientific stuff. But I figured out a lot of other things on my own—like what 'fellatio' and 'cunnilingus' mean." Her mouth stumbles over the long words. "And 'sodomy'."

"So? What does your big vocabulary have to do with me?" I eat my second pastry, watching her carefully and keeping my face blank.

"Theo, I know what you and Jonathan do, and I think Della and Dad are about to figure it out too." She eats another handful of popcorn, not looking away.

My jaw is still moving, chewing my food, but I can't taste it. I make myself swallow and take a drink of milk. "And what is it you think I do with Jonathan?"

She sets the bowl of popcorn aside and pulls her knees to her chin. Her low-cut jeans and midriff shirt reveal way too much skin for an eleven-year-old girl. "I know you're gay, and he's gay, and I've heard you two in here when you thought no one was around."

"Sounds like you've been hearing a lot lately."

"Theo, I don't care what you do..."

"Why are you telling me this? What do you want?"

"First of all, I thought you might want to know." She hesitates. "And second, I wanted you to finally owe me."

"Great." I lean my head back against the wall. This is a revelation. She is wrong, because Jonathan and I don't actually DO anything, but her little pre-pubescent brain got part of it right. "Okay. Tell me."

"It's mostly Della. She was hysterical—I heard Jonathan's name several times—and Dad kept telling her to calm down."

"Typical."

"He was telling her everything would be okay."

When Samantha doesn't say anymore, I try to think. "Is that it?"

"Yeah."

"You're sure."

"Yes. I'm sure."

"So, what do you want?"

"Your old magazines."

"What?"

"I've seen the stash you've got under the bed."

"You are way too young, and anyway, Della will find them."

"I already thought of that. When Kate spends the night, you slip two magazines under my pillow, and after she goes home, I'll put them back."

"So, you only want them when Kate is here?" I need Sam on my side, so I don't say anything more, and I don't laugh.

"Well." She squirms and moves toward the edge of the bed. "Not exactly, but I haven't figured out how to keep Della out of my room."

"How 'bout a lock?"

Her face lights up in a smile. "Would you help me?'

"Yeah," I say, realizing that a lock on her door is probably what she wanted all along. My sister is doing the same thing—looking at naked guys in magazines—that I did when I was eleven, but she seems so much younger. Weird.

Dinner is quiet. Samantha stays through dessert. I try not to meet her eyes too often. Having her as an accomplice feels strange—it keeps me from teasing her about the mashed peas stuck in her braces.

My dad and I wash dishes while Della clears the table. Samantha helps and then waits at the kitchen counter until Kate's mom honks from the driveway. I focus on each plate and fork and cup that I hand off to Dad. I don't want to break the silence left by Samantha.

When the last dish is finally done and the counters are wiped clean and there are no more reasons to stay in the kitchen, I dry my hands.

"Guess we're through here," Dad says. He doesn't use his cane inside the house. He presses the walls with his fingertips and teeters slightly as we walk to the living room. Della is waiting in the blue wingback chair on the far side of the coffee table. Dad picks the chair next to her, so I sit by myself on the sofa. The leather cushions squeak when I pull my feet beneath me.

"Theo, you know why we're here?"

"Sure." I pick something from my sock.

"Why?" she asks.

"Because you're worried about me."

"And?"

"And… I don't know."

"Let me refresh your memory."

Here, Dad puts a hand on her forearm and she hesitates. "Theo, we *are* worried about you…" Dad says. He clears his throat, distracted by something on the arm of his chair.

"So I hear." I dare to look at Della, but her stare on me is hard. I look at my lap again.

"Theo, we know you spent some time alone with Matt on the trip…" Dad's voice trails off again.

I don't respond, so Della forges ahead, disregarding whatever agreement she's made with Dad to let him do some of the talking. "Your father said that you and Matt were very awkward around each other yesterday." She pauses. "Theo, please look at us when we talk to you."

My chest feels like it is wrapped in a canvas strap and someone has just pulled the wench a notch tighter. I raise my eyes and try to empty my face of all emotion.

"We would like to know what happened between you and Matt on the trip." She leans forward in her chair.

"Nothing happened."

"I saw you two talking on the bridge," Dad offers. "What were you talking about?"

My face feels hot. I've got to give them something or they won't let up. "We talked about the fort, about high school… friends he had in college."

"What kind of friends?" Della asks.

"His roommate was big into working out." I start making shit up, hoping to lead them away from where they are trying to go. "He ran track in college and was saying how he'd always tried to run with his roommate but could never keep up."

There is a long silence, and then Della asks, "Why was it so odd between the two of you when you saw him at the laundromat?"

"I don't know." I try to think faster. "I was just tired, and probably neither of us really wanted to be there."

"Did you ever talk to him about being gay?" Della asks.

I look straight at her and answer without looking away. "No, we didn't talk about that. It's not usually something I tell someone I don't know very well."

"But you would tell someone you *do* know well… like Jonathan?" She stares at me, unblinking, unflinching.

"Yes," I say slowly.

"And when did Jonathan tell you he was gay?"

I shrug. "I don't know. A long time ago." I look at my dad, trying to gauge if the part about Jonathan is his fight, too. Dad is quietly staring at his hands. I look at Della. "I've known for a long time, but he's not my type."

"Oh? I didn't know you had a type." She sits straighter in her chair. "Last I heard, you weren't interested enough to have a type."

Shit. "You act like I'm supposed to tell you every detail of my life."

"I wouldn't call sexual attraction a detail."

"But it *is* private." I put both of my feet on the floor. My hands are pressing into my thighs. "If I'm attracted to someone or not, that's my business." The words come out too loud.

"Theo, it's more complicated than that," Della says. "If you were interested in girls—"

"How is it more complicated?"

"Theo," Dad says after a moment of silence. "It's more dangerous for a young gay person to be sexually active than it is for a straight person." I try to cut in, but Dad keeps going. "Hear me out, Son. We know AIDS isn't confined to gay men, but it is much more likely for gay men to be HIV positive than almost any other segment of the population."

I hold my breath.

"Emotionally, forming homosexual relationships can be difficult and result in a lot of pain, probably more than heterosexual relationships."

"You sound like a book. Have you been reading parents-of-gay-kid-manuals or something?" My hands are shaking and my voice is shaking too. I feel like a specimen, not a son.

"Actually, we have. This is *terra incognita* for both of us," Della says. "That means unfamiliar territory."

I bite my lip so I won't scream at her that I'm not stupid, and I swallow, and I make myself stare at the coffee table.

"We're worried about you, Theo."

Della's voice is softer, but I can't stop myself. "I'm gay. I'm not mentally challenged. You're treating me like I'm a freak that you need to diagnose with some special handbook. Just leave me alone—I'll let you know when I need your 'expertise.'" I stand to go. "I'm going to my room."

"You need to tell us what's going on so we can help you."

"I don't need help." I spin around. "I'm not sick. There is nothing wrong with me." I run my hands through my hair, pulling hard.

Della and Dad look tired and small and sad. I stare from one to the other. "I'm going." I walk away and take the stairs two steps at a time, fighting the urge to slam my door. I lie flat on my bed and stare at the ceiling, and then I pull the pillow over my head and howl into it. Minutes. Hours. Days.

Jonathan is only a phone call away, but I can't stand the thought of being listened to, accidentally or not. When I hear Samantha close the front door, I turn off my light and throw my jeans, socks, and T-shirt to the corner of the room. I slide under the covers. Moonlight slants across the carpeted floor, and I listen to an old Pink Floyd CD on continuous play until I can no longer keep my eyes open. Wouldn't it be easier to be a lunatic on the grass? If I were crazy, surely I wouldn't feel so awful. So guilty.

CHAPTER SIX

A chilly wind is scattering clouds across the sky and hurling them toward sunrise. The undersides, looking like rippled sand after high tide, are dotted with gold and orange. It reminds me of the beach near Fort Pickens.

I can take my time. I left early, left a note for my parents. I am finding back streets, small hills to scale, time to think.

I stop near a tall chain-link fence. It surrounds the public pool where Jonathan and I used to swim. We showed off for each other, back dives and front flips from the diving board. We chased nickels and quarters beneath the ropes that mark off the deep end. I always had coins. Dad and Della required that I call them every few hours. I was first in line at the pay phone when the lifeguards blew the whistle for break. Jonathan liked to pour ice down my back or dunk my towel in the pool when I was on the phone. We spent the summers doing stupid pranks. Sam was our target. I hated her. But she was a trooper. It was only after Dad's accident that she started running to Della with everything little I did. Della takes Sam out of school every week now to see a counselor. Maybe that's a good thing. Maybe the porno magazine alliance means Sam is done with her tattle-tale phase.

I leave the pool, realizing I might be late for school. I'm a few blocks away when the first bell rings. I eat two breakfast bars on the way to Burnett's class after locking my bike. Every seat is taken except for the empty desk beside Jonathan. I set my backpack on the floor and slump in my chair unnoticed because Burnett is already scrawling explanations on the board.

Jonathan nods at me. "What's up?" he says.

"Too much," I say.

For lunch, we drive to a nearby park and sit in Jonathan's truck. The only other vehicle is a black jeep backed into a space in the next lot, the driver staring out through dark sunglasses. He waves at us. Perv.

Jonathan waits until I've eaten one of two turkey sandwiches his mom made for him before asking about the big conversation.

"It sucked." I take another bite. "They think I'm a science experiment or something. Like they have to protect me by reading all these manuals."

"I'm not following."

I finish the sandwich and wipe mustard from my cheek. "They asked tons of questions about Matt. About you. Then my dad—my dad who is *brain damaged*—starts in on this shit about how being a homo is dangerous and I'll probably get AIDS or have my heart pulverized if I have a 'physical relationship' with anyone."

"At least he's not trying to talk you out of being gay."

"It's like they've got to handle me with latex gloves."

"Maybe they're just worried."

"Of course they're worried, but they act like I'm an idiot and I'll never figure out anything on my own." I eat one of Mrs. Norton's chocolate chip cookies in a single bite. "Whose side are you on, anyway?"

"Your parents', obviously." Jonathan rests with his cheek on his forearms, which are crossed over the top of the steering wheel. He watches me eat a third cookie. "I guess it's a good thing I brought extra."

"Sorry." My mouth is full. "I forgot to make my lunch." I put my trash into the plastic bag on the seat between us, grabbing whatever Jonathan has left there too. "Your mom's cookies are the best."

"Why don't you sleep over tonight?"

"Unlikely." I take another cookie and eat it slowly. "How do you know," I ask, "that your parents have no idea you're gay?"

"No way," Jonathan says. "You know my dad... he'd be the first one to throw a punch if he thought one of his sons was queer."

"Your mom?"

"She'd keep it to herself."

"What if your dad figures it out?" I know what will happen, but I want to hear Jonathan say it.

"He'd try to beat it out of me, and then I'd go live with Brian."

"In Columbia?"

"Yeah."

"So Brian knows?"

"He knew before I did." Jonathan smiles. "And he knows better than I do what it feels like to disappoint the old man. He's felt the lash of that belt more than once." He leans back into the bench seat. "What have you told your folks about me?"

"That you're not my type."

"Is that so?" He turns his body toward me. "Is Matt your type?"

I stare out the windshield. "Not any more." I reach across the gearshift to check the time. "He's old. And confused."

"A winning combination," Jonathan says.

"Yeah. I want someone young and available. Right?" I try to sound sarcastic. I try to look at him. "Someone who knows he's gay."

"You'll find him." He looks away and starts the truck. I roll down my window and throw the garbage into a green

55-gallon drum with *City of Springfield* spray-painted in block letters on the side.

"What will you do?" Jonathan asks. He pulls away from the park, leaving behind the guy in the black jeep.

"Assert my independence."

"You mean rebel?"

"Yeah," I say. "That's what I mean."

"That'll be a first."

"Thanks."

He laughs. "Basketball tonight?"

"And the sleepover too. Might as well go all out."

He is quiet for a minute. "What if Della decides to have a little talk with my folks?"

"That would suck." I slump against the seat.

"Fuck," he says quietly.

"They don't understand about your dad."

"What about my dad?"

"That he's…" I swallow. "That he's violent."

"Nobody understands that." He finds a parking space and turns off the truck. "Your house. 4:30."

I want to ask him to come earlier. "Right," I say.

"See you," he says and disappears into the crowd.

By late afternoon the sky is overcast. The air is gray, that bright kind of gray when squinting behind sunglasses isn't enough.

Jonathan is waiting on the bleachers after practice. The team is huddled around Coach Eberhardt, a slight, soft-spoken guy. He went to college with Della back east. He used to come to our parties before the accident. Awkward. It was weird to already know Coach before I was in high school, but I tried out for the track team anyway. I appreciate that Eberhardt doesn't treat me any differently than the other runners.

He dismisses us after reading out race assignments for Saturday's meet. I move toward the bleachers, walking beside Donovan. Coach insisted on putting us together for stretches at the beginning of practice. I couldn't focus. I almost rolled my ankle twice when we ran together as 'buddies' through town. Donovan runs shirtless. Every time we wait at an intersection for the light to change, I stare at the traffic, at storefronts. Anywhere but at Donovan. When we are actually running, though, I can count the freckles dotting his shoulders.

Jonathan isn't alone. Richard is sitting next to him. "Hey, Theo."

"Hey," I say. Richard looks like he's been in the Caribbean or somewhere exotic for spring break. He has a deep coppery tan and his hair is streaked with blonde. He's wearing a choker, shells woven in every few inches.

"I thought you were going to meet me at home." I put my foot on a bench, stretching forward. I'm fucking horny from the run with Donovan.

"Richard needs a ride," Jonathan says. "I thought you could use one, too." His elbows are on his knees, chin resting on his hands. He seems to be enjoying the view of all my partially clad teammates gathering their things from the stands. Or maybe he's just lingering in the afterglow of a blowjob from Richard.

No.

I pull up my sweats over my shorts, and the three of us walk toward Jonathan's truck after I unlock my bike from behind the bleachers. Jonathan takes the bike from me and pushes it through the parking lot, walking between Richard and me. We thread through the few cars left in the lot near the tennis courts, Richard asking Jonathan about his next soccer game, about the basketball game tonight. We stop at Jonathan's truck, and he swings my bike up into the bed. His triceps ripple as the bike arcs through the air.

The truck is unlocked, so Richard gets in while Jonathan loads the bike, sliding to the middle. Of course. He gets to sit mashed up next to Jonathan, the gearshift between his legs. I throw my bag in back next to my bike and sit pressed against the door, my leg and hip and shoulder hot and sweaty. I have to touch Richard because the space is so tight.

I don't want to talk. They do, though. They joke. They laugh. They discuss soccer tryouts in the fall. Graduation. They are both juniors. I am a lowly sophomore. I seethe and stare out the window.

Richard's two-story house is in an older neighborhood. It's sided with dark wooden shake, hemmed in by overgrown red cedars and boxwood bushes brushing up near the foundation and double-hung windows. It's a real fixer-upper. I thought Richard was wealthy, but maybe not. The place is kind of charming. I might like it if I liked Richard.

When we get to my house, Jonathan leaves the truck running, and I ask too many questions about Richard.

"I won, didn't I?"

"What?"

"The bet."

He rolls his eyes. "Move on, would you?"

"You're not going to tell me?"

"There's nothing to tell."

"Fuck there's not."

"Back off," he says.

I unload my stuff. He doesn't get out of the truck.

"Are you coming in?"

"No."

The house is quiet. It's another half-hour before my parents get home, and Samantha is probably at Kate's. A few months ago, my dad would have been home at this time of day. He took lots of naps, but after winter break, he stopped getting rides home in the afternoons and managed to stay awake all the way through dinner. Yes, I'm glad he's on the mend. Of course I'd feel shitty for disobeying Della if Dad were still hobbling around the house in a daze needing her constant attention. I have tried to do everything right since the accident—study hard, run hard, help around the house. But being a good boy is getting old.

I grab clothes for tomorrow, leave a message on the counter, and lock the front door. I get in Jonathan's truck and slide on my seatbelt. I wipe my face on my t-shirt. Damn, I need to take a shower.

Jonathan backs the truck out of the driveway.

"We're going to your house?"

"Nope."

"Where?"

"It's a surprise."

I decide to shut up for a while so maybe we'll stop arguing.

After we pass several frat houses and apartment complexes, we enter a quiet neighborhood. Jonathan turns into the driveway of a wood clapboard house with a stone chimney. A holly tree is growing on the far side of the front door, and river stones wind from the driveway to the cement steps. "Whose house is this?"

"Guess." Jonathan pulls up to the garage door and then turns off the truck.

I won't guess.

"It's Tom's house," he says.

"Why?" A knot coils in my gut.

"He's a nice guy, he likes both of us, and I thought he might have some ideas about how to handle our parents." He taps my leg. "I'm sure he's been through this before."

"You hardly know the guy."

"Yeah, and this is how we get to know him—hang out for awhile, get comfortable, ask his advice."

"Or see if he's up for a threesome?"

"Well, maybe." He smiles, at last. "Let's go before he thinks a couple of crazies are parked in his driveway."

"Yeah, we wouldn't want him to think we're weird."

We get out together and stand awkwardly before the door while Jonathan rings the bell. Loud music hums from inside. Jonathan pushes the button again just as the handle begins to turn.

"Hey, guys!" Tom opens the door, a pale blue business shirt unbuttoned at his neck and a glass in his hand. He is grinning. "What brings you to my neck of the woods?"

"Just driving by," Jonathan says, his hands stuffed in his pockets and his voice a bit tight. "I told Theo you had a sweet place." He looks at me.

"Right," I say, noticing the wood floors and carefully painted entryway. I wasn't expecting something this nice.

"Come on in," Tom says and holds open the storm door for us. I catch the faint scent of his cologne as we pass. A candle is burning on a dark oval coffee table, offering up little smoke compared to the cigarette perched in an ashtray nearby. Tom grabs the ashtray and uses the remote to turn down the stereo. "I'll just put this out in the kitchen," he says. "I try not to indulge in my bad habit when I have guests."

We stand in the living room. The fireplace is empty of logs and instead contains several candles on tiered iron holders. There are framed pen and ink drawings of men's hands on either side of the mantel. Behind the sofa, a tapestry of a black park bench and red hat woven into a stark white background hangs on the wall.

"You guys want anything to drink?" Tom calls from the kitchen.

"Sure," Jonathan says. "Got any soda?"

"In the can or over ice?"

Jonathan looks at me. "Over ice," he calls back.

"Comin' right up."

There's a loveseat set at an angle from the sofa. Jonathan makes himself comfortable. I sit on the sofa, across from him. "I gotta take a shower," I say, pulling my shirt away from my skin. It's damp. I don't want to mess up Tom's furniture. "Ask him if I can use his shower."

"You ask."

I stare at him.

"He won't bite."

"How do you know?"

"You're just nervous."

Tom comes in and hands drinks to each of us. He sits next to me and spreads marble coasters across the coffee table. He leans back and looks from Jonathan to me.

"Well, boys?"

I clear my throat.

"Um," Jonathan says. "Theo is wondering if perhaps he can use your shower… I sort of kidnapped him from track practice."

Tom takes a sip of his drink. It looks like soda, but it smells like whiskey. "Kidnapped?"

"Yeah," I say. "I'm sweaty." I'm an idiot.

Tom takes another sip, and this time, I can see his lips curl into a smile. I look away.

"Got a change of clothes?"

"In the truck."

Jonathan throws me his keys. "No funny stuff," he says.

Tom shows me the bathroom. Bedroom doors on either side of the hallway are open, one revealing a dresser covered in coins and keys and small objects, an unmade bed, clothes on the floor, and a guitar upright on a stand. The other room is spotless—a double bed, computer, a bookshelf full of books, more framed artwork on the walls.

"Have a roommate?"

Tom is getting a towel and washcloth from the closet. "Used to," he says. "Now it's just the guest room."

"Is that your guitar?"

"Yep." He sets the towel on the counter. "I'm in a band."

I'm impressed. He wears a string choker, like Richard's, but looser. "What kind of music?"

"Some old rock covers, but mostly originals… kind of alternative country/rock." He straightens some magazines on the back of the toilet and lights a candle on the counter. "You play?"

"I wish."

The bathroom door closes behind us, and I'm standing too close to him. The room feels small. I look at the reflection of the two of us in the long mirror over the sink. "I guess I'll take a shower."

"Right," he says. "Feel free to use the toiletries." He smiles and taps the countertop.

"Thanks." My arms are crossed. I'm clutching my clothes to my chest. We switch places on the tiny cotton bathmat and then he leaves.

I stare at the mirror and quietly lock the door.

Jonathan and Tom aren't glued to each other when I finish my shower. They are still clothed, talking and laughing together on the sofa. I found Tom's cologne and put some at the base of my neck. Asian grass and white tea. I tried to memorize the brand.

"Much better," Jonathan says.

"Thank you." I set my bundle of dirty clothes in the entryway.

"Where are you going?" Jonathan calls.

"Setting my stuff by the door." I come back to the living room. I sit by myself on the loveseat and sip my soda. It doesn't smell like whiskey.

"Was the shower alright?" Tom asks. "I forgot to tell you that sometimes when the washer kicks into rinse, the flow dribbles down to about nothing."

"No," I say, "it's fine." I put my glass on the marble coaster and sit back. No one says anything.

"We've been talking about you." Tom leans forward. He tells me Jonathan's been describing my parent troubles.

I look anywhere but at them.

"Theo. Don't." Jonathan reaches across and puts his hand on my shoulder.

"Everyone's parents are different," Tom says and takes a sip of his drink. "It sounds like your family's had a rough year." He balances his glass on his knee. "And it's hard when they act like they don't know what the hell to do with you because you're gay."

My parents have probably seen the note by now and are discussing me at this very moment.

"How long have they known?"

"A few years."

"But they don't know anything," Jonathan says.

"They've been asking questions." I pull my legs up to my chest and wrap my arms around my shins. "And my little sister's been spying on me." I look at Jonathan. "She thinks we're having sex."

The statement hangs in the air.

"Are you being careful? Condoms?"

We both say yes. However, I can't imagine a blowjob with a condom. Sex, sure, but it's not like I'm going to lose my virginity soon.

"Would things change if your parents knew you were sexually active?"

"His parents would get over it," Jonathan says. "Unlike my parents..."

"Yes?" Tom says.

Jonathan hesitates. "My dad's an asshole sometimes."

"Sometimes?" I say.

Jonathan's face goes red. I don't say anything more.

Jonathan sits up straighter. "My dad wants to know when I'm going to bring home another pretty girl like Ellen."

"Ellen?"

"His one go at straight sex," I say. "His dad would have been apeshit happy."

Tom looks at me. "And *your* parents?"

I am quiet. Tom has his feet up on the table, which I want to do, but I forgot to bring extra socks. I dig my toes into the carpet. "I don't know."

Jonathan jumps in, saying how my parents have all of these rules and shit. They're lame. I'm a teenager and they don't even know it. "It's been crazy over there since the accident. But they don't see it." He looks at me. "Who forgets their son's sixteenth birthday?"

I flinch. He is making my family sound ridiculous.

"Your dad's accident," Tom says. "That's some scary shit."

"Yeah," I say. I look at the clock on the mantel. I'm starving. "We gotta go, Jonathan. The game has already started... I need some food."

Jonathan doesn't look like he's ready to go anywhere.

Tom says his band is coming over tonight to practice, but we're welcome to stay as long as we want. He puts his nearly empty drink on a coaster and settles again into the cushions, perhaps just a little bit closer to Jonathan.

I'm not sure if I want to stay, but I'm not sure if I want to go, either. I'll start being an ass if I'm hungry for too long. Tom offers to treat us to Chinese buffet.

"Sure," Jonathan says. And so do I.

The restaurant is crowded, a place near Tom's house with over three hundred items to choose from and free drink refills. He is buying. Jonathan and I wait in line for Mongolian bar-be-que. "We can't go back to his house," I say.

"Let's skip the game." Jonathan holds out his plate and the chef loads it with noodles and meat and vegetables. Jonathan waits with me for my food. "I know you like him," he says.

"That doesn't mean I want to have sex with him."

A few heads turn. Jonathan leans in. "He's not Matt."

"I don't want to watch you giving head."

"Then I'll watch you."

The chef loads a pile of beef and broccoli onto my plate. I leave and Jonathan follows. He doesn't get it.

Tom is working on his second helping of sesame chicken and noodles. "What did they cook up for you boys?"

"Veggies and beef," I say.

"Beef," Jonathan says. Tom and I get it at the same time. We laugh.

Okay, so maybe it wouldn't be so bad.

At Tom's house after the meal, Jonathan calls his mom and tells her he'll be late and not to save any dinner. There is no mention of any calls from Della.

I am on the sofa and Jonathan is on the loveseat. I listen while Jonathan lies to his mother on the phone. Tom is in the bathroom. Jonathan sets down the phone. "Ready?"

"No," I say, but Jonathan nudges with me with his foot, punches my arm. He knows I've given in.

We reach an agreement. He'll do the work, and I'll relax.

Right. At least it will be over soon.

When Tom returns, Jonathan disappears with him behind the wall separating the hall from the living room. I wait. I light the candle on the coffee table. I let the match burn almost to my fingertips. Smoke curls slowly from my hand. There is no ashtray, so I go to the kitchen and run the match under some water in the sink. I look at black and white photographs on Tom's wall showing various stages of the erection of the Eiffel Tower. I stare until Tom comes up behind me.

"Been to France?" he asks.

I step aside, making room for him to stand closer. "No, have you?"

"Used to go a couple of times a year with my boyfriend."

"I didn't know you had a boyfriend."

"We broke up a few months ago." He touches the edge of one of the frames. "He's a great guy. It took us a long time to figure out that we weren't really compatible."

I lean against the counter. Jonathan is in the living room, giving us some time alone. I can do this. "How did you figure it out?" I ask.

"We argued a lot. He never went to see me play music." He pauses. "And the sex, it just wasn't right for either of us. We get along better as friends."

I look at the Paris photos again.

"Hey, let's go downstairs." Tom touches me on the shoulder. "I'll show you where the band practices." He opens a door just off the edge of the kitchen and leads the way down a wooden staircase. Oriental carpets are draped along the concrete walls. A full drum kit surrounded by free-standing wooden drums and microphones takes up most of the central floor space.

"Sweet," I say, resting my hand on one of the drumheads. It looks handmade.

"That's a *djimbe,* from West Africa. You hold it between your legs." Tom sits on a stool and leans the drum back into his lap. "So the sound can resonate through the bottom." He taps a rhythm, repeats it, and then sets the drum back. "My thing is guitar and vocals," he says. Three guitars are propped on stands, two electric and one acoustic. He scoops up a stray cord and begins winding it around his arm. "Sorry for the mess."

"No," I say. "This is great."

"My boyfriend always said I don't want to grow up, but it keeps me happy."

I stand near the drums. I rest my fingers on the edge of a *djimbe.*

"You could try it," Tom says. "It's user-friendly."

"I'm not very musical."

He is sitting on a stool near the guitars. "Jonathan said you wanted to talk about something."

"He did?" I put my hands in my pockets.

"It's okay," Tom says, "if you don't really want to talk."

"Well, it's not exactly that." I can't help but run my hands through my hair. It's becoming a habit. "Jonathan seems to think I need to expand my horizons."

Tom nods, interested.

"He's been meeting guys lately." I don't know how much to say. "And I was with this guy in Florida." I shove my hands back into my jeans. "I tried to seduce him." I move to a stool and lean against it.

"And you got turned down?"

"Not quite." I stare at the floor. "I gave him head. Then he lost it and punched me."

"That's awful!"

"Yeah." I look up, surprised at the anger in Tom's voice. "Well..." I'm going to explain how it was my fault, but the words won't come. I sit on the stool with my hands in my pockets, remembering how Matt's voice sounded when he cried.

Tom comes and stands near me. "Hey, it's okay." He puts a hand on my shoulder. "No one should ever treat you like that."

The knot in my stomach pulls so tight that I gasp for breath. Tom just stands there, waiting. Can I relax? My face burns, heat rising to my cheeks like it always does just before I'm about to lose it. I rub my hands back and forth on my thighs. I wipe the back of my arm across my face. How fucking embarrassing. Tom sits on the steps. Close, but not so close that I have to get up and walk away.

He looks like he has all the time in the world to sit there and wait for me to get myself together.

I laugh. "Jonathan didn't bring me here to talk..."

Tom smiles and waits for me to finish the thought. But I can't.

"He wants a threesome," he says.

"Yeah." I wipe my face again.

"He means well." Tom shifts his feet on the stair. "It's a confusing time. Sex has a way of making all the pain go away... for a while." He stands and leans against one of the beams supporting the floor overhead. "Don't get me wrong. I don't know any guy who would turn down the chance at an evening with the two of you."

I try to smile.

"But it would be a lot more fun if it was something you really wanted, too."

I can imagine putting Jonathan's plan into effect. "I do like you," I say. I'm standing and trying to hold my voice and my legs steady.

"Then call me sometime when you're ready," Tom says and pulls me into a hug. It feels safe and warm and like a place I could stay for a long time. I bury my head into his shoulder and breathe.

Jonathan is watching music videos, sprawled across the sofa and looking like he might have fallen asleep. He rubs his eyes and yawns. I sit by him, and Tom stands beside me.

"Anything exciting happening up here?" I ask.

"No," Jonathan says. "Anything exciting in the basement?"

"You mean you didn't hear us?" I say.

Jonathan looks at me, then Tom. "What did I miss?"

"Oh, everything," Tom says. "But maybe we'll give you a repeat performance sometime." He sits on the armrest. I lean back, playing along, and Tom drapes his arm across my shoulder.

"Why not right now?"

I stifle a fake yawn. "Too tired."

"Seriously?" He swings his legs around to push off the sofa but I shove him back against the cushions.

"Give it up, you whiny ass. Nothing happened."

"Nothing?"

"Zip," Tom chimes.

Jonathan looks back and forth between us and shakes his head. "Great."

The doorbell rings. "Come on, I'll give you the full details on the way home," I say, pulling Jonathan off the sofa.

"You guys don't have to go."

"Yeah, we should." I start inching toward the door with Jonathan. The doorbell rings again.

"Alright," Tom says. He looks at me. "Call me."

"Hey." Jonathan moves between us. "What about me?"

"This is for you," Tom says and kisses Jonathan hard on the lips, and then pulls away. "I've got to answer the door." He holds Jonathan's hand and leads him to the entryway. I follow them. Tom kisses Jonathan again and says, "You can call me too."

In Tom's driveway, Jonathan starts grilling me. "Well?" he says. "Did you kiss?"

"No."

"Then what'd you do?"

"Talked. He showed me his drums."

Jonathan drives, taking his eyes away from the road occasionally and watching me in the darkness of the truck cab. "What'd you talk about?"

I relax into the seat, leaning slightly toward Jonathan with my head resting near his shoulder. "Matt."

"What about him?"

"Nothing specific."

"Come on."

"Mostly good stuff."

"Like what?"

"Like… no one should ever treat me like that." I rest my hand near Jonathan's leg. "He didn't really say much. He was nice, and he didn't make me feel like a moron. He's not a counselor or something, is he?"

"No, he works for a bank."

"He's got nice stuff, nice clothes… and he smells nice too."

Jonathan shifts gears as he turns onto the gravel road. He puts his hand back on the steering wheel.

"I don't know why you're pushing so hard for something to happen," I say.

"I think it would be good for you."

"You're good for me," I say, and I move away from him, toward the door.

"No, I'm not," he says, and he turns on the radio. His face glows in the lights from the dash, but he doesn't want to talk, and now I don't want to either.

Mrs. Norton is waiting for us. "Is that you, Jonathan?" she calls from the kitchen. "Is Theo with you?"

"Yeah, Mom."

"He needs to call Della." She's drying her hands on a dishtowel. "Hello, Theo."

"Hey, Mrs. Norton." I'm trailing Jonathan into the kitchen, wishing we could have slipped in unnoticed. "Did she leave a message or anything?"

"She wants you to call her right away."

"You can use the phone in my room," Jonathan says. "Mom, we're going to study and then call it a night, okay?"

"Sure, Hon." She stays near the counter and takes a moment to flatten the dishtowel. "I put the leftovers from supper in the fridge."

"We already ate, but thanks, Mom." He kisses her on the cheek. She is too quiet.

Enter Dr. Norton. "Well if it isn't the dynamic duo."

"Dad."

"Son."

"Dr. Norton."

"Theo."

"We were just going down to finish some homework." Jonathan nods his head toward the stairway.

"How's your father these days?" Dr. Norton is staring at me. He is smiling, but he stands in that legs spread, arms akimbo stance that says *answer me*. "I don't see him much now that we're out in the sticks," he says.

"Better every day," I say. Since the accident, Dad has forgotten that he once disliked Dr. Norton. The man yells at his sons—shouts and rants that can be heard through the walls and windows, even in winter, when the houses are closed up tight. But now, Dad seems to like him, laughing at the cutting jokes, not realizing they are often at his expense.

"Hate to see a good man brought down like that," Dr. Norton says.

I don't know what to say.

"Not the shining star he used to be, is he?"

I look at Jonathan. "Homework," Jonathan says. "We've got homework, Dad."

"Yes, Hon, let them go," Mrs. Norton says from the counter.

"Excuse me?" He turns to her. She looks small.

"Goodnight, Boys." She looks at Jonathan, then me.

"G'night, Mom," Jonathan says.

"Goodnight, Mrs. Norton."

We nod at Dr. Norton. His arms are now across his chest. He squints his eyes and nods. I skim down the stairway with Jonathan, as if we are making a narrow escape.

Jonathan stands at his doorway, shaking. His father's voice echoes down the stairs until I close the door.

Jonathan's room is still packed—half-opened boxes stacked randomly, pushed up near the wall or stranded in the middle of the floor. Clothes and a trophy poke out of a box near the door. I sit next to it on the carpet and lean against the wall.

Jonathan disappears into the bathroom, and I watch the door close. I pick up the phone, key in my home number, and cross my legs and push my back into the wall. The answering machine picks up, and then I hear Della's voice. She is fumbling with the buttons. I wait.

"Della?"

"Theo? Are you at Jonathan's?"

"Yeah. Mrs. Norton told me you called."

"Since when do you leave a note on the counter informing us that you'll be spending the night with a friend?"

I don't answer.

"I specifically asked you not to make any plans with Jonathan."

On cue, Jonathan walks in and sits across from me. "You don't need to worry about me." *Such a bitch.*

"You need to come home now."

"I'm staying here."

"No, you're not."

"We've got to study for an exam tomorrow."

"Theo."

"What?" I shoot an imaginary pistol at the phone.

"Your father looked for you at the game." She pauses. "He got there during the first quarter and waited until the game was almost over."

I can't conjure any brilliant lies. "Jonathan picked me up from school and we drove around awhile, then we got some dinner, then we came here."

"That's three hours, Theo."

I don't want to argue. "Look, Della. We weren't doing anything wrong."

She is quiet for a minute. She is breathing into the phone, but she doesn't say anything. I wait. Finally, in a very quiet voice, she says, "Theo, when you come home from practice tomorrow, I want you to stay here until your father and I get home." When I don't say anything, she adds, "Do you understand?"

"Sure."

"I expect to see you."

"Okay," I say and hang up. I sigh and rest my head against the wall. "Fucking pain in my ass." I stare at the bare glass of Jonathan's windows, the reflections of the empty walls and corners of Jonathan's room.

Jonathan lies lengthways across the mattress on the floor. "She needs to lighten up."

I don't want to talk about my parents. "Tell me something I don't know, asshole."

"You're a shitty liar."

"Shut up."

"They both treat you like a baby. You let them run your life."

"Oh yeah, I'm not the one trying to fuck girls so my mom and dad won't figure out I'm a fag."

"This isn't about me."

"Yeah, right," I say.

"Whatever," he says. He kicks at my legs. "Do something."

"Fuck off." I shove him away.

"Make me," he says and kicks at me again.

I grab his leg and hold it, twisting. We struggle, rolling across the mattress. When we stopped moving, I'm on top. "Give up?"

"No," he says. He stares into my eyes and breathes slowly. "You?" He shifts my weight to the side, and we are wrestling again, but this time he finishes on top. I'm face down, arms pinned behind my back.

"Give up?" he asks.

I try to twist from his grip.

"I think you'd best give up." He leans forward, pressing his weight against me, pushing his crotch hard into my ass. He keeps my arms pinned with one hand and with the other reaches under me and starts undoing my zipper. "Is this what you want?"

"No!"

"Too late," he says, his lips near my ear. I yell at him to stop, to get the fuck off, struggling against his full body weight pressed into my back, my ass, my legs.

In a very quiet voice, he says, "No."

My chest is heaving. He is undoing his jeans. He has a button fly that gives way one button at a time. This isn't going to happen. I struggle free and get on top again. I hold his arms out to the sides, staring into his eyes, trying to figure out where the hell my best friend has gone.

"What are you gonna do now?" he asks.

"I'm gonna kick your ass," I say and pin both of his arms under my knees.

"You can't do it."

"I don't see you stopping me."

He shifts his legs. "I'm just letting you think you're in charge."

"Fuck you," I say and backhand him across the jaw. "What the fuck is wrong with you?"

He is stunned for a second. He looks up at me. "My best friend's a pussy, that's what."

"Yeah, well my best friend's a slut and an ass."

He strains against my knees. "You're a coward, Theo." He swings his legs all the way to my shoulders and pulls me backwards. My body slams to the floor, and then we scramble. I finally kick him away and stand, and when he lunges, I punch him, making solid contact with his left eye. He drops to his knees, holding his head in his hands. I push him backwards, digging into his body.

"You stupid motherfucker!" I swing over and over, sending uppercuts to his ribs, his chest, until finally, I realize he isn't giving any resistance. I stop and he pulls away, hunched, cradling his head. I watch his shoulders heave.

He sits back on the mattress, and I lean my weight into the wall, alert in case it isn't really over. He is bleeding but I don't want to touch him.

"Why the fuck did you do that?" I ask.

He tries to pull at his shirt. He finally gets it loose and wipes his eye. Blood stains the fabric.

"Why did you do that?"

"I don't know."

"I hate you."

"I wanted to see if you could kick my ass."

"Now you know."

"Yeah. I know."

My hand aches and I hold it in my lap. I straighten my pants and try to zip them. My fingers tremble.

Jonathan wipes his eye again and winces. "You win," he says

I can't look at him. It feels like I have lost. I start running my good hand through my hair, pulling until it hurts, and then pulling some more.

Jonathan shifts to his knees and moves nearer. "Don't touch me," I say.

"I'm sorry."

"No."

The skin below the edge of his eyebrow is turning bright pink.

"I was stupid," he says.

I hold my clenched fist. My chest is burning and I keep breathing too hard. He sits next to me, sighing heavily into the wall.

"I'll get some ice," I say, and I go upstairs. I fill a small, plastic bag with cubes from the freezer door and find a hand towel. All of the lights are off except one over the kitchen sink. There is a reflection in the French doors—a shadowy figure with tussled hair and wrinkled jeans hanging off one hip. I stare at myself in the dark glass, imagining Jonathan behind me, fucking me up the ass.

I grab a bag of chips, two cans of soda, and an entire bottle of ibuprofen.

Jonathan is on the bed, lying curled on his side, both arms tucked under his head like a pillow. He looks like he is dreaming.

"Jonathan?"

"Mmm." He shifts his body to the edge of the bed.

I set the towel filled with ice in his hand and kneel beside the mattress. "Here," I say, holding two pills. I wait for him to sit upright. I don't want to look at him, and I don't want to touch him, but I can't help but stare at the outline of swelling tissue around his eye. It reminds me of what my dad's eye looked like when they first changed the bandage.

"Shit hurts." Jonathan's face twists from the effort of trying to swallow. He groans and lies back on the mattress. "See my pillow?"

"Here." I turn off the light and arrange the bed for him and set several blankets for myself on the floor.

"That's too far."

I don't want to be near him, but I tuck the blanket around his shoulder and tell him to move over. I lie on top of the blanket next to him and hold the ice to his eye. His face is all in shadow, only a hint of light coming from the bathroom.

"I'm sorry," he says.

I don't answer.

"People won't push you around if you don't let them."

"I didn't need you to try to fuck me up the ass to figure that out."

"I told you I'm not good for you." He moves his arm, puts his hand on mine. "I'm sorry."

"I know," I say.

He is quiet, and his breathing is silent, like he isn't breathing at all. I wait for him to say something else. I look at the shadows near his face.

He moves again. Sound, but not quite words, escapes his lips.

I let go his hand and pull the covers higher over his shoulder. I draw my arms in tight to my chest, my fingers clenched. I don't want to feel the skin on his body, the skin I bruised and bloodied with my own hands, my own rage.

"I'll stop being with other guys" he says.

"I don't care," I say. "I don't care." I turn away from him and sob. I hold my arms tighter to my chest. I can't stop. Jonathan puts his arm around me and tries to hold on.

It's not about other guys. It's not about fucking. It's about dying. Killing someone with your own rage, not even knowing you were angry.

A long time passes but I can't sleep.

Jonathan moans every once in awhile, hanging in some balance between dreaming and pain.

"Don't leave me," I whisper into the darkness.

"Never," he says.

CHAPTER SEVEN

The room is beginning to glow with morning. When the knock comes on Jonathan's door, it takes me a while to realize where I am. The knocking comes again, more insistent.

"Jonathan, are you up?"

"Yeah" he mumbles.

"It's almost seven. You want a lunch today?"

"Sure."

"What about Theo?"

"Yeah."

"I'll leave them on the counter." The second stair creaks with Mrs. Norton's weight, and it sounds like she is gone, but then there is another tap on the door. "I'm putting a load in the washer. Anything I can put in for you?" The knob starts to turn.

I roll off Jonathan's mattress, my heart pounding. I pull a blanket up to my chest.

"I'll do some laundry later," he shouts. "Fuck," he whispers.

The knob stops. "Don't be late for school," she says. The stair creaks again, and this time her footsteps go all the way up to the kitchen.

"You need a lock."

"No shit." He tries to shift his shoulders, but stops. "Damn."

The skin near his left eye has split and deepened to purple. "Nice color," I say. I am fascinated by the swelling along his cheekbone. And repulsed.

He touches his eyebrow with a tentative finger. "Shit."

"Ice?"

"Please."

I pull on my jeans and go upstairs. Mrs. Norton is gone, and so is Dr. Norton. Two brown lunch sacks sit side by side on the counter. Della hasn't made my lunch in years.

Jonathan and I are quiet with each other. He moves slowly, but doesn't ask for help. I don't know what he remembers saying last night, or if any of it was true. We don't talk in the truck.

At school, time stretches into a slow, boring, eternity. I eat in the cafeteria. I sit with guys from the track team and try to participate in their conversation, but I'm not interested in tits and ass talk, or who is the easy lay of the week. I listen quietly to their stories and no one notices that I don't want to go out and get some ass for myself.

Coach works us after school, singling out slackers for extra pushups and laps. I run hard so I won't have to stay late, so I can get home before my parents. Eberhardt's pep talk for the upcoming meet is uninspiring. I like the guy, but it's all I can do not to bolt before he finishes his diatribe.

My bike is chained to the rack outside school. Jonathan can't give me a ride. The soccer team has their first spring game soon, and he's staying late the rest of the week to practice. My ride home is chilly, my clothes damp because I didn't stay to shower and change into something dry.

No one is home. There is a folded newspaper on the counter and a pile of mail. And two envelopes full of photos. I pull out the pictures—a few are from the weekend we went sledding in February, but most are beach and campground shots from Florida. I set aside the close-ups I photographed of flowers and grasses along the beach. I stop when I get to pictures from the night of the potluck dinner. There we are, Matt and I, side by side—arms almost touching. Matt is smiling.

I pull out three more pictures, two of Matt on the beach and one of him walking alongside my dad. I stare at the cane. It was carved by a guy who lives a few hours north of Springfield in a little river town called Rocheport. My dad and I floated in a canoe on the Missouri River in the autumn before his accident, a few weeks after the Chiefs game and the Rufus Wainwright concert. The departure point on the river was in Rocheport, near where Lewis and Clark traveled on their way west to find the ocean and begin mapping the country three hundred years ago. The tour guide also led canoe trips on an underground river in the caves beneath Rockbridge State Park. My dad and I were scheduled for late March, before the little grey bats woke for spring. When the tour guide called to confirm, Della explained the accident. The cane showed up in a box on the doorstep a few weeks later, long before Dad was ready to use it. Now, it goes with him everywhere.

I leave the picture of Matt and my dad in the stack on the counter and take the other photos to my room, along with the phone book and my backpack. There is no listing for 'Matthew Clay.' He didn't move here until July, after he was hired by Dad's department. I dial information and an electronic voice gives me Matt's number. I write it on the back of one of my spiral notebooks, minus the name.

I key in the numbers and wait, hoping for a recording of Matt's voice. I listen to the message four times before I finally set the phone down. Samantha will be home soon, full of questions and information, and my parents will be home not long after. I lie back on my pillow, staring at the constellations pasted on my ceiling. The phone rings just as my eyes are closing. It is a man asking for David, my dad.

I ask if I can take a message, and the guy says, "Yes, Theo. It's Matt."

Silence.

"Your number is on my caller ID," he says.

"Yeah," I say, trying to clear my throat.

"What's up?"

"I wanted to talk."

"Okay," he says.

"Can we meet?" I run my fingers through my hair. They ache from last night.

"Is that a good idea?"

"I need to talk to you."

"Did you tell them?"

"No," I say.

"You should tell them."

"I need to see you," I say. "I need to talk."

He doesn't say anything. He takes a breath. "Okay," he says.

"Tomorrow?"

He rustles some papers. "Sure."

"11:30 at Ebbet's Field."

"Do you want me to come get you?"

"No," I say. I can ride my bike.

"Fine," Matt says. "I'll see you then." And we hang up.

I lie there with the phone on my chest. Lunch. Tomorrow. I have less than twenty-four hours to figure out what I will say.

I am almost done with chemistry when the garage door starts grinding open. Dad and Samantha are coming up the driveway in the van—without Della. I close my book and decide to hang out in the kitchen, test the waters to see how bad things really are.

"Hey, Theo," Samantha calls.

"Hey, Sis." I shuffle through the photos still on the counter.

She comes up next to me, looking over my shoulder, and then whispers in my ear. "You're in big trouble."

"Tell me something I don't know."

"Della was crying last night."

"Great." I say. I would ask for more details, but Dad comes in from the garage.

"See ya," Samantha says, and she sprints around the corner and up the stairs.

"So glad you decided to join us, Son." Dad sets his briefcase and a bag of groceries on the counter. "Della will be glad to see you."

"I doubt it." I stare at the pictures one at a time. "Need any help?"

"Sure. Leave out the vegetables and the pasta, though. They're for tonight's dinner."

"Grilled vegetables and pasta?"

"Yep," he says, unloading folders from his briefcase onto the dining room table. "I decided it's time to take over some of the workload from Della."

"Can you add some meat?" I set the milk in the fridge and put a box of penne on the counter. "Dad?'

"Yes?"

"What about some meat?"

"What about it?"

"With the vegetables," I say. I place the bags of zucchini, peppers and onions next to the sink.

"Sure," Dad says. He sinks into a chair and rubs his knees. He pats the table. "Come sit."

I fold the paper bag, taking my time.

"You should have come home last night."

"I needed to be away for awhile."

"Theo." Dad rests his chin on his hand. "You do still live here, and there are rules you have to follow."

I lean back in my chair and cross my arms in front of my chest.

"Della is worried sick about you, and so am I."

"There's nothing to worry about," I say, exhaling too much.

Dad puts his hands on the table, on the papers and folders he's taken out of his briefcase. "I called someone today."

"Who?"

He clears his throat. "I called a gay helpline, and then I called a counselor."

"Come on!" I push my chair away from the table. "So I can work on my little gay problem?" I pace behind the counter.

"It's not a problem that you're gay." He clasps his hands. "The problem is if you're sexually active."

"It's not like I went out and picked up some guy in a bar."

"What *have* you done?" He looks at me. "Did you use condoms?"

"Would you stop! Just stop, okay?"

"Stop what? Stop caring about you? Stop worrying about you?"

"No. Stop treating me like I'm stupid, like I'm some stupid kid that has this problem and can't figure out anything on his own." I shove my hands in my pockets to try to keep from running my fingers through my hair.

"But you're not on your own, see? Sex can be dangerous, and you're my son and I'm scared of what I see you doing."

"And what is it you think you see me doing?" I put my hands on the counter and lean forward.

"I see you taking risks," he says. "I see you trying to prove to anyone who will listen that you aren't a kid anymore."

"Right. I'm not a kid anymore. I'm glad someone finally fucking noticed. Ever since the accident it's 'Be careful this, be careful that.' Just because *you* got hurt, that doesn't mean *I'm* gonna get hurt." I hear the front door open—Della. "I'll be up in my room." I start to walk away and then look back.

"You can send Della up to interrogate me whenever you like."

"Theo—" Dad says, but I'm already up the stairs before he says anything else.

I wait in my room until Samantha comes and tells me dinner is ready. When she taps on the door, I'm sitting on the edge of the bed with my head in my hands. I've never yelled at Dad since the accident. I'm sick of being quiet. Of always trying to be good.

"Theo?"

"What."

Samantha pushes the door open. "Dinner's ready."

"Great."

"Dad sent me up to get you." She perches on the bed next to me.

"Go away, alright? Just tell him I'm not feeling well."

Samantha waits a moment, and then stands to go. "Come on, Theo. Don't make me eat alone with them again." I don't answer. She squirms a bit, digging her toe into the carpet. "Don't wait too long, okay?"

After she leaves, I listen to the downstairs dinner preparations. I go down the steps and take a deep breath when I get to the final stair. In the kitchen, Dad is stirring a pan on the stove, leaning on the countertop to balance with his free hand. Samantha and Della are already seated.

"Hello, Theo," Della says. Her eyes skirt away from me, and she sips her ice water.

"Hey," I say. I take the napkin from under my silverware and flatten it across my knee. Her eyelids look red and swollen.

"Here we are," Dad announces, setting the bowl of pasta in the middle of the table.

Here we are. Joy and happiness.

We eat to the clinking of metal and silence. The knuckles on my right hand feel stiff, and I struggle to hold the fork.

"I got my science test back today," Samantha says.

"How'd you do?" Della asks, dabbing at her chin with a cloth napkin.

"B plus."

Sam is trying. I attempt a smile, but my lips feel like wood.

When Della doesn't say anything, Dad says, "That's wonderful, Sweetheart."

"Thanks," Samantha says. She goes back to spearing her vegetables.

"Enough meat for you, Theo?"

"Sure, Dad. Thanks." I take another bite, stifling a snort. Samantha's fork drags across her plate like she gets it too. I look up at her.

"You find that funny?" Della asks.

"No." Our eyes meet briefly, and then I shovel food into my mouth to keep from saying anything more. I clutch my napkin under the table.

"You know, this isn't a game, Theo. You're hurting all of us."

I look at Della. My cheeks burn. "Why do you make it about you?"

She takes a slow drink of water. "I don't believe I said 'me.' I was speaking for all of us." She motions her glass to Dad and Samantha, and then takes another sip.

"I'm not hurting anyone here," I say. I look at Samantha. Her face is white.

"Yes, you are," Della says.

"It's normal that I want some privacy."

"Samantha, maybe you should leave the table."

Samantha hesitates.

"Samantha."

"I know what's going on, probably more than you."

"Is that so?"

I look at Samantha again, her arms crossed over her chest.

"Yeah," she says.

"And what do you know?"

"Um..." She drops her eyes to her lap, realizing her mistake. "Nothing," she says.

I look away. I don't know how strong our new alliance is.

"So," Della says to me. "You think what you're doing doesn't hurt any of us?"

I don't say anything.

"When were you planning to mention that your best friend is gay?"

"Della, let's save this for later. Okay?"

My hands are shaking. I can't take another bite—I might puke across the table, all over her face. "Like I said," I put my fork down. "You turn things around so they're about you. So what if Jonathan's gay? What the hell does it have to do with you?"

"You will not use that language, and it has everything to do with me. I expected more from you. You're sixteen years old, Theo. I expect you to make better choices while I'm taking care of your dad."

Dad and Samantha are staring at their plates. I am in this alone. "Della, this isn't about you. Or Dad. Or Sam. It's about me! It's my life!"

"Theo, sit down," Dad says.

"No." I stare at Della across the table. "Stop trying to control me. Stop trying to use Dad's accident to make me feel guilty. He got hurt, you took care of him, and now he's better. Get over it."

"Don't you walk away from this table!" she says.

The door from the kitchen to the garage slams behind me. I duck under the garage door with my bike.

"Theo, come back!" She is standing inside the garage.

"Fuck off."

I pass under streetlights, pedaling through the chill of evening. I'm only wearing a T-shirt and jeans, and the temperature is dropping. I keep aiming my bike along back streets, pedaling harder and faster each time I think of Della's face across the table, or the top of my dad's head, bent over his half-empty dinner plate.

I slow down in a neighborhood bordering the college campus. I'm shivering. I let go of the handlebars to blow on my hands, trying to keep them warm. I recognize the huge old houses that have been converted into law offices and apartments. This is close to Tom's house. Across the railroad tracks and two streets over, then about five blocks down. Maybe I should have called Tom today instead of Matt.

Shit. Lunch tomorrow with Matt.

The street is dark, a light overhead only every fifth house or so. I accidentally pass Tom's place and turn back when I get to the cross street that connects to the business district. I make a wide arc with my bike and ride slowly, scanning each house on the right. They all look familiar, but then I see the stone chimney and the holly tree. I lean my bike against a pin oak closer to the sidewalk. There is a truck parked in front of the garage. I've never seen Tom's car. I click my bike lock into place, and I walk over to the truck, thinking it looks a lot like Jonathan's. Low lights are on in the front room of the house and there's music. I can hear someone talking. I get to the passenger door of the truck and freeze. It's Jonathan's. The stupid troll with pink hair that I hate is hanging from the rearview mirror, and fast-food trash is piled on the floorboard.

My armpits tingle and I can't stop saying *fuck, fuck*. After walking around in circles, I lean against the truck and bend forward, hands on my knees and blood pounding in my head. Someone is laughing inside the house. It's Jonathan. I want to get on my bike and ride away, but where else can I go?

I rub my palms on my thighs. I push away from the truck and shove my fingers into my pockets. The doorbell button glows next to the storm door. I rest my palm on the wood siding a moment, then press, listening to the faint chime that follows.

Tom opens the wooden door in his bare feet. "Hey, Theo." He pushes on the storm door and holds it open. "Come on in. You must be freezing."

I am numb inside and out. "I was just in the neighborhood...."

"A little cold to be riding without a jacket, isn't it?"

"Yeah." I hover near the threshold. On the other side of the entryway, I will be able to see into the living room.

"Let me get you a sweatshirt." Tom nods his head toward the next room. "Jonathan's here."

"I saw his truck in the driveway."

Tom puts his arm around me. "Come on."

Jonathan is sitting on the sofa, a glass in his hand, the outer edge of his left eye dark and swollen.

"Look who's here," Tom says. He pauses, looks at Jonathan, at me. "Let me get you that sweatshirt," he says.

My hands are balled into tight fists in my pockets. I wait, rigid and trembling, watching the doorway where Tom has disappeared.

"Surprised to see you," Jonathan says. He puts his feet on the floor and sets his glass on a coaster.

"Likewise," I say. I inspect the candles below Tom's mantelpiece.

Jonathan clears his throat. "What brings you?"

I look at him. "The same reason you're here." I stare at the Oriental carpet, the wood floor. "I needed someone to talk to," I say, quietly. I want to say something mean, but nothing comes. I lean against the mantel with my arms across my chest, watching Jonathan. With the swollen eye, his face looks off-balance.

"Sit down."

"I'm not going to stay long," I say. I watch him to see if he is relieved, but he is blank. "I should get home."

"None of that, now," Tom says, holding a grey sweatshirt. "You just got here." He hands it to me. In navy blue lettering, *Columbia College* is spelled out across the front. "My alma mater," Tom explains. "A soccer scholarship. Let's make you something warm to drink… hot tea?"

"Nah," I say. I take the warm fabric and hold it a moment, then slide it over my head. "My folks are probably worried."

"Your folks are always worried," Jonathan says.

"Yeah, that's what you keep telling me." I pull the fleece material down to my waist.

"Please stay," Tom says. He pulls me toward the loveseat.

"I should get going," I say, but I let Tom pull me. I sit on a cushion. I am cold.

Tom leans back and spread his arms, one on the armrest, and the other along the back of the loveseat behind me. "At least stay here until you warm up a bit," he says.

Jonathan relaxes into the sofa, staring at the coasters on the coffee table. I watch him.

"That's quite a shiner you gave ol' Jonathan," Tom says. "I take it you boys had an argument."

"You could say that." I shiver and wrap my arms across my chest.

"We were arguing about his parents," Jonathan says.

"Jonathan seems to think I should stand up to them. But he hasn't told you about his dad, has he?"

"Don't," Jonathan says.

"Okay," I say. "Have you ever gone against his wishes?"

"I do it all the time. He just doesn't know."

"Just because my dad won't beat the shit out of me doesn't mean I need to 'stand up to him'." Jonathan's face is immobile. "My dad called a hotline today. He says he's trying to figure out what's wrong me."

"But he knows you're gay," Tom says.

"That's not the problem," I say. I look at Jonathan. "It's sex. I'll get sick. I'll hurt myself." Something dull aches low in my gut.

"Do they know where you are now?" Tom asks.

"No."

"It sounds like you're standing up to them." Tom looks at Jonathan. Jonathan rolls his eyes.

"I don't care what he thinks," I say. I stand to leave. "I've got to go. Thanks for this." I grab the neck of the sweatshirt to pull it off.

"Keep the shirt," Tom says. "And stay awhile. You don't have to go so soon."

"Yeah," I say, looking at Jonathan. "I do."

Tom follows me to the front door and out onto the lawn. "You don't have to go. I could ask Jonathan to leave."

"No, he was here first." I reach down to unlock my bike.

"Theo," Tom touches me on the shoulder. "You and Jonathan have something special."

"We had something," I say, snapping the U-lock into place.

"He's your best friend."

"Things change." I lean against my bike. "You shouldn't keep him waiting." My throat is so tight I can barely get the words out.

"I'm sorry, Theo."

"Yeah, so am I." I swing my leg over the bike seat and roll across the grass. I coast down the driveway.

"Take care," Tom says.

"Thanks," I say. Enjoy my best friend.

There are lights on at home. I ride into the driveway of the empty house next door—Jonathan's old house. I bring my bike around back and hide it behind the bushes near the patio and then check to see if the window in the garage is locked. It doesn't have a screen. I test the window, and it slides open. I have to pull myself up and heave my body over the sill. I close the window. I jiggle the handle on the door that leads from the garage to the house. Still loose.

The house is dark, the only noise coming from the refrigerator. A twelve-pack of soda sits inside on the second shelf next to a half-empty water bottle. I pull a can from the box and press the metal tab into place.

The rooms feel cavernous. Most of the curtains are open on the windows that face the back yard. Light filters in from outside, but not enough to penetrate the corners of the rooms. I sip my drink and walk slowly up the carpeted steps. I turn left to Jonathan's room. I kneel near one of the windows and pull up the blinds—my room is across the yard. The light is on. My parents are probably going through all of my stuff, trying to figure out why I am such a lost cause.

I think all of the times I've stared into this window that I am now kneeling in front of. Coded flashlight messages, magazine photos pressed to the glass. When Jonathan isn't physically present, he is in my head. He was with me every step of the way in Florida, cheering me on. Everything I've ever known about sex is tied up with him. But he can get turned on by anyone, wants to get turned on by anyone. Tom. Guys at the park. At the public library. On the dance floor at Martha's Vineyard. He is leaving me behind.

I set the soda on the sill and lean my back against the wall under the window. I lie sideways, almost exactly where I would be if Jonathan's bed were still here, if he were here. I tuck my hands under my head and scan the walls in the semi-darkness, imagining Jonathan's posters, the bulletin board over his dresser filled with movie stubs and film negatives arranged to spell out the obscene word of the week, the photo collage he made the summer after 8th grade of the camping trip when the two of us got lost in the woods near the Buffalo River in northern Arkansas. Intentionally lost for the first hour, but hopelessly, really lost for the last three or so hours until we finally heard my dad slapping his paddle on the water.

That camping trip was the first time I wanted something more from Jonathan. At night, we went to the river by ourselves. If we were quiet and the adults were sufficiently drunk, no one noticed when we slipped away. After the episode of getting lost, I didn't want to let Jonathan out of my sight. When I couldn't talk him out of crossing the river, I followed him and sat on the far gravel bar watching fireflies and waiting for shooting stars. Some nights, the streaks of light cross the sky every few minutes, and sometimes not at all. That night, we waited a long time before spotting one, but it was worth it because the tail stretched across the entire black space of sky above the river. I turned to him and said I made a wish. But I couldn't tell him what it was.

He was always older, stronger. He didn't look at me the way he looked at other guys, the way I looked at him. Last night, after the fight, I thought maybe things were changing.

Light pours through the window and floods the opposite wall. I'm awake. I don't sit up—there's too much light. I edge up to the window. The front light is on and the back porch light. The light in my room is actually off. I almost move in front of the window, but then I realize I wouldn't be able to see if there is anyone in my room across the way watching me—they'd be in darkness, and I would be fully lit.

My parents must be worried. I don't have a watch. It can't be that late. I crawl to the doorway and glide down the stairs. The clock over the oven says 9:57. Maybe I fell asleep.

I leave through the door from the dining room to the garage, then out the window. It's shielded by a thick Norway pine, so I'm covered in shadows. When the window is in place, I listen for a full minute, and then decide to free my bike from the bushes. I get to the end of Jonathan's driveway without hearing any alarm go up, so I ride away from his house, and then double back around the block.

Our garage door is open. I ride my bike inside and set it against the far wall. I hit the button and the door grinds downward, and then I take a breath and open the door to the kitchen. Dad and Della are both sitting at the dining room table, just like I left them. The dishes have been cleared and the flat space of the table is bare. They both look up when I enter, but neither says anything. Della is holding something in her hands, something metal that she keeps turning over in her fingers. My dad gets up and dials the phone. "Sheila, Theo's come home… Yes, I'll call you if we find anything about Jonathan." He hangs up the receiver. "You have some explaining to do."

I close the door and hesitate near the fridge. "Why'd you call Mrs. Norton?"

"Why'd you run away?" Della asks, her hands closed around the shiny object. She looks up. "Why did you lie to us?"

My dad leans against the wall, clears his throat and folds his arms across his chest. He doesn't say anything to stop her tirade.

I am unable to take a step further. Unable to speak. I plant myself and lean into the refrigerator.

Finally, Dad pulls a chair away from the table and sits down, his face heavy with exhaustion. "We thought you might go to Jonathan's, so we called, but Jonathan hasn't been home all evening." He drums his fingers on the table. "Did you see him?"

"No," I say. I wrap arms around my chest. "I was just out riding."

"That was a long time to be out riding," Dad says. "Where did you go?"

"Just around."

He nods. "And the sweatshirt?"

I forgot about the shirt Tom gave me. "I borrowed it from Jonathan a few days ago. I left it on my bike so I'd remember to give it back."

Della looks up and studies the lettering partially hidden under my arms. "And who does he know that goes to Columbia College?"

"Some friend of his brother's."

Della sits there, lips slightly parted, silent. She stands slowly and moves toward the counter. And then she tells me that until my behavior changes, I am grounded to my room except for school—she'll be bringing me to and from school. She'll be talking to Dan Eberhardt to let him know I won't be running for the team anymore.

I can hardly breathe. *You bitch, you fucking bitch.* I would say this if I could speak.

Dad speaks for me instead. He argues with Della.

"Let's talk about it, Hon. You're being a little harsh."

"No," she says. "I'm being fair. I've been making all the decisions on my own, but if you can do better, then do it."

They argue back and forth, the first time since the accident. The tight feeling in my chest, like I can't take a deep enough breath, reminds me of their fights before the accident.

"I expect to see you waiting on the driveway at 7:10 am," Della says to me. I've slowly shifted back toward the fridge, hoping they'd forget about me, but Della is staring so hard that I just stand here, frozen. "Goodnight to both of you," she says and starts to leave. She stands in the hallway and says without turning, "I'll be sleeping in the guest room, David, so don't wait up." She gives him the shiny metal thing she's been turning over in her hands, and says he can decide what to do with it. And then she is gone.

Dad sits there, silent and still, and then he motions toward the empty chair. "I think you should take a seat, Son."

"I want to go to bed, Dad. It's late."

"No, I've got a few things to say."

I move around the counter and push the seat away from the table. I fold my arms and try to look at him, but I can only stare at the floor.

"Della… this is tearing her up inside."

"Come on."

"Hear me out, Theo. I was your age once. Even though I've forgotten a lot since the accident, I can remember what it felt like to be a teenager, horny twenty-four/seven, and ready to be rid of my parents. You know, Della put a lot of trust in you because she thought you could handle yourself. She *needed* you to handle yourself responsibly… but you haven't. Being gay doesn't give you license to have a secret life—"

"You can't tell me you told your folks everything."

"No," he says. "I didn't, but I also didn't give them reason to worry."

"Because you never did anything wrong?"

"Well, perhaps I was more discreet, but I didn't have as much to lose as you do. Times are different now, more dangerous."

"Dad, you've said this already."

"I know, and you never want to hear it. But this time, you need to listen." He pauses. "I've always felt at a loss as to how to help you—"

"I don't *need* help—"

"I mean *guide* you. When we, your stepmother and I, realized you were attracted to boys, I wasn't angry, or repulsed."

"You really don't have to tell me all of this."

"I know I don't, but I'm telling you anyway. So be quiet and listen, okay?" He holds his hand to his right temple, near his scarred cheekbone, on the side that always gives him headaches.

"Fine," I say, looking at the floor again.

"When we found out, I was lost, like I'd been thrown a curve ball and I realized too late that my old man had never shown me how to swing at a curve ball."

Great. A story.

"Your grandpa and I had never been all that close, but when he died, I was only twenty, and we hadn't spoken to each other in over a year. I pissed him off, and we were both wrong, but neither of us would apologize. I made a promise to myself, listening to the priest and friends and family—everyone but me—list off all these ways he'd been helpful and strong when they needed him. Your mom was there. She knew what it was like. When I made this promise to myself, I guess I promised her, too." He looks away a moment.

"If we ever had kids," he starts again, "I was going to do right by them… sort of a way of saying sorry for being an ass and not realizing my father was a good man despite all the shortcomings I saw in him. And to show your mom—I hadn't proposed yet—that I would be a good father to our children. That's part of why I gave you this watch of his." He looks directly at it and hands me the shiny metal object Della had been holding. "He died and I never got the chance to tell him thank you."

"For what?" I hold the watch, wanting to know why it wasn't hanging by my computer, but afraid to ask.

"That part you'll have to figure out for yourself, maybe when you've got your own kid."

"I probably won't be having any kids, Dad."

He takes a deep breath. "I hadn't thought of that… You know, I sometimes think I've failed my dad, because I can't give you what he gave me… because you're gay, which seems to make you so different."

"Dad—"

"But really you're not so different than I was as at sixteen," he says. "If I'd had a best friend that was a girl, I can see how it might have turned into more than friendship…"

"Jonathan?"

"Yeah."

"We are just friends. That's it."

"You don't have to tell me," he says. "It's not him I'm worried about."

"Then who?"

"Matt."

"Dad, nothing happened with Matt."

He frowns and sits thinking a minute, his finger resting again near his temple. "Theo, are you sure?"

"Of course I'm sure."

"Alright," he says through a sigh. "Go to bed." He yawns and stretches. "You weren't with Jonathan tonight?"

"No," I say. "I wasn't."

I go upstairs and collapse on my unmade bed. I hold Grandfather's pocket watch to my chest. What would my mom think if she could see me now?

CHAPTER EIGHT

Samantha's knocking wakes me at 6:45am. I forgot to set my alarm. "The bathroom's open," she calls from the hall.

I groan. "Thanks."

The water is hot, and the shower feels good. I lean forward into the spray with my head down, watching the stream fall from my chin to the drain. No bike. No track....

I squeeze the shampoo into my left hand, remembering the medicated green liquid at Jonathan's house. Jonathan. I consider skipping first hour so I won't have to see him. After Mr. Burnett's class, it will be easy to avoid Jonathan. That would please Della.

Della is silent and cold on the drive to school. Samantha sits up front with her. I don't move forward when Sam gets out. Della has to drive the last mile like a chauffer.

"I'll be here at 2:30," she says, staring out the windshield, hands clutching the steering wheel.

"Great," I say.

She turns and looks at me. "I expect you to be here, at the front entrance."

I don't say anything as I grab the door handle and push the door closed, and I don't look at her. I walk away, losing myself in the crowd. *At the front entrance my ass*. I made a commitment to the team. I will be at practice, and if she wants to find me, she can come looking for me.

It is so early that Burnett isn't even at the chalkboard when I take a seat. There are sometimes a few empty desks in the far corner of the room, as if the janitors go a little crazy and shift desks from one room to another and lose track of what goes where. I consider sitting in the corner. But no, I set my backpack in the usual spot. My homework isn't finished—the call from Matt interrupted my power nap between assignments. Lunch. With Matt. In less than five hours. I get out my textbook, notebook, a pencil and my calculator. I try to lose myself in the equations, but the sound of shuffling feet is distracting.

There is a cough, and then a slow deep breath. Jonathan has entered the room. I focus on each digit on my calculator. Black sneakers come into my side view, frayed jeans and Jonathan's green backpack with the Rufus Wainwright button I gave him. I am tracing the shiny black lettering with my eyes. I look back at the lines on my notebook paper.

Burnett scratches on the front board with his chalk and his voice begins droning in its familiar monotone. Finally, I look over at Jonathan, his darkened left eye.

Meet me for lunch, he mouths.

I don't say yes or no. I let my eyes fall to Jonathan's hands, and then to the floor. I can't make myself say no, but I sure as hell can't say yes. Matt will be waiting for me at 11:30.

Jonathan folds a piece of paper and slides it onto my desk. MEET ME FOR LUNCH. I scribble underneath that I have plans and hand it back. AFTER SCHOOL, Jonathan writes. PRACTICE, I write. He writes AFTER PRACTICE. I write OKAY.

Passing notes. I reach over and take it from his desk and crumple it. I shove the paper in my pocket and then try to pay attention to Burnett's painfully boring explanations of the homework problems. I want to scream and run, but I can only sit here and listen to Jonathan's slow breathing.

At the end of class, I gather my books and leave. I get to the end of the hallway when I hear Jonathan.

"Wait up," he says.

I turn and let the crowd split and stream around me. I watch Jonathan's face. I want to throw my books at him and shove him into a locker. Instead, I stand there calm and still.

"What are you doing for lunch?"

"Meeting a friend."

He is puzzled. He knows who all of my friends are, and the list of names is pretty short. "Who?"

"Nobody," I say. I shift my backpack and watch students walking by. I don't want to give in.

"Did you go home last night?"

"Yeah."

"My mom said your parents called."

"Yeah." I don't want to ask, don't want to know when he got home last night. "The bell's gonna ring," I say.

He touches my forearm. "I'm sorry about last night," he says.

I lift my arm away and take a step back. He has never done this. "Forget about it," I say. "I gotta go."

The next three classes are even more painful than Burnett's. I stare at whatever my eyes settle upon, a window, the back of a boy's head, a wad of paper on the hard tile floor. My mind drifts from one face to another. Jonathan, Matt, Tom. I have no idea why I asked Matt if we could meet for lunch. I don't care anymore. Maybe it was a crush, but now it is nothing.

The front entrance is empty. Students leaving school grounds for lunch usually go through the side doors near the parking lot. I look for the blue hatchback, don't see it, settle myself near a brick wall. My stomach is caving in on itself. Shit. I told him we'd meet at Ebbet's Field.

I start walking, hands in my pockets and head down, feeling like a stupid ass. It will take fifteen minutes to get there on foot. Matt will be relieved if I don't show.

After the third block, a horn honks at me from across the street. "Theo?" It's Jonathan.

"Hey," I say. He pulls the truck to the curb and I cross over.

"Where you headed?"

"Up the road." I shift my backpack.

"Lunch?"

"Yes."

"Want a ride?"

"Sure," I say.

"Where to?" he asks, pulling away from the curb.

"Back that way." Jonathan makes a U-turn. We come up on an intersection and Jonathan slows.

"Which way?"

I sigh. "Ebbet's Field."

Jonathan waits for cars to pass and then turns left. "Where's your bike?"

"Remember how Della was trying to ground me?"

"Yeah."

"She did. Last night when I got back from... Tom's house. No bike. No track."

He looks at me.

"Let's not talk about it." I stare out the window, wishing I said no to the ride.

"Who's the mystery person?"

"Matt." I slump down into the seat and pull my knees up to the dash.

"A date?"

"No," I say. "I don't know what it is."

Jonathan drives several blocks and then pulls over and turns off the truck. "This is it," he says.

"Great."

"Look. I'm really sorry about last night, about Tom's."

"You wouldn't be apologizing if I hadn't shown up."

"I should have talked to you first."

"You're free to do what you want."

"I know, but… Did you say Matt has long hair?"

"Yeah."

"I think I see him."

I sit up. Matt is standing on the front porch to Ebbet's Field, a renovated older house turned into a bar and grill with a baseball theme. Faded pennants hang from the eaves, frayed and fluttering in the chill breeze. "Fuck." Matt hasn't seen us yet.

"You didn't tell me he's gorgeous."

"You think?"

"Of course."

"Shit. What am I doing?"

"I don't know." Jonathan leans forward over the steering wheel. "How about I go with you and we fuck with him a bit."

"No."

"I owe you this."

Matt looks our way. He sees me.

"I don't think so," I say.

"Come on. I won't be too hard on him… but he does deserve a little punishment."

"He didn't do it," I say. "I did."

Matt is walking toward us.

"Alright," I say. "But nothing too weird."

"Right," Jonathan says, and we both get out.

"Hey, Matt." I close my door. "This is Jonathan."

"Hi," Matt says. He holds out his hand to Jonathan. His gaze lingers on Jonathan's swollen eye. He is wearing a long-sleeved, light peach button down shirt and jeans. His hair is pulled back into a ponytail.

"You still have time to eat?" he says. He checks his watch. "It's almost noon."

"Yeah," I say, and the three of us go in together.

To say it is awkward wouldn't be saying enough. I almost trip on the steps, and then a strand of pennants catches on my shoulder and comes unattached from one of the porch columns. It's dark and smoky inside, tables covered in red and white vinyl gingham. I'm stumbling over myself like a kid going through a growth spurt. I want to leave.

We wait near the door for a table. "I was surprised you called," Matt says to me.

I'm looking around, spacing out. "Yeah," I say.

Jonathan talks. "So, Matt, you work at the university?"

"I'm a postdoc. Got a fellowship to try to turn my dissertation into a book."

"Mathematics?" Jonathan asks.

"Yes," Matt smiles. "Is it obvious?" He looks down at his shoes.

"Nah," Jonathan says. "Theo told me. My dad's in the History Department."

The waitress steps between us to grab menus and then tells us to follow her.

"Does this table work?" she says.

"Looks fine," Matt says. His voice is like a delicate thread that I want to wrap around my neck and tie into a noose. Jonathan is good at the small talk. He can deflect Matt's bullshit.

I stare at my menu.

"Hey... Earth to Theo," Jonathan says. "Want to order anything?"

"Sure," I say. It feels like I'm in a dream and Matt and Jonathan are the repeating images that make no sense. "No breakfast this morning."

"You must be starving," Matt says.

"Yeah," I say. Smoke from nearby tables wafts our way. I'm going to smell like I've been out drinking. Again. Maybe I should just skip the rest of the afternoon. Avoid teachers' questions. Della. But if I miss practice, I won't get to run in this weekend's meet. That is, if Della hasn't already talked to Coach.

Matt orders a burger with fries and a soda. I'm going to order the same, but I say chicken sandwich. Chicken for a chicken-shit. Jonathan orders a burger. I want to call the waitress back.

Matt and Jonathan are talking, some bullshit about string theory and the golden ratio. I get enough of that kind of stuff at department events. The topic of Jonathan's black eye hasn't been mentioned. Music filters to our part of the restaurant, weaving through curling haloes of smoke. The tunes are rock classics. I am humming. I remember where I am and stop myself before the words actually leave my lips.

The waitress brings glasses of water to the table, which gives me something to do. I crunch melting cubes with my molars and watch Matt run his finger along the drops of water accumulating on the outside of his glass.

There is a lull in the conversation, and Matt turns to me. "How's it going with your parents?"

I keep chewing, thinking. "I don't know what the hell is wrong with them," I say. "They're both being bitches."

Jonathan laughs and Matt clears his throat. "That's hard to imagine," Matt says.

"For you, sure. They put on a front for you."

"They're probably more formal in public. Most people are like that."

"Then most people are assholes."

"Here, here," Jonathan says. He raises his glass. "To all the assholes."

I join him with a loud gulp.

Matt leans forward and sips his water. "Your dad called yesterday."

Jonathan nudges my leg under the table and then pushes his chair back. "I'll be back," he says.

"Right."

Matt watches Jonathan leave.

I sink into my chair. I weigh a thousand pounds. "What did you say to my dad?"

"He left a message, and I haven't called back… yet."

"Fuck," I say, choking. My stomach is devouring me from the inside. I take a few more drinks of water. I wish the damn waitress would come back with my soda.

Matt rests both of his forearms on the table, like he's going to pray, or confess. "Theo, I'm really sorry—"

"Yeah, well, maybe I'm not," I say. "Maybe I wanted more." Prickles sting my armpits.

Matt's eyebrows are up, opening his face into an expression of surprise, or maybe fear, that I recognize. The waitress inserts herself between us, setting down my drink first and then Matt's and Jonathan's. She lingers, flirting. Not with me, but with Matt. *The bitch has no idea.*

I sip my soda, willing myself to be calm.

"Maybe I should clarify," Matt says. Then there are a few moments of silence dulled by the noise of people talking, glasses clinking, music. He speaks quietly. Slowly. "I'm sorry for my emotional outburst, Theo, and the way I pushed you. That was incredibly wrong, and stupid."

I watch him, afraid if I speak that I might laugh or cry or yell. I swallow the words creeping up the back of my throat, like *fucker* and *pussy* and *I love you*… All of it stupid shit like that because what the hell do I know about love? I lean forward and whisper, "What about the part in the fort?"

Matt breathes. "I made a mistake."

"Your mistake is messing with my head. Okay?" My voice is too high.

"Have you—" Matt hesitates. "Have you told anyone?"

"Yes," I say, watching Jonathan and the waitress approach the table. "I told him," I say. Matt looks up and then looks away. Jonathan stands and waits while the waitress sets the plates on the table.

"Anything else?" she asks, hovering near Matt.

He looks at me. "No," he says. "I think we're fine."

Jonathan sits. "Did I miss anything?"

I pour ketchup on my plate. "Not much."

The three of us start eating.

Jonathan says to Matt, "I don't think you realize what an impression you've made on Theo."

Matt looks from Jonathan to me. "What is it you want from me?"

Jonathan turns to me. "Yeah, Theo?"

I sit back in my chair. I am gulping for air.

Matt is staring at his water and lifts his glass to take a drink.

When I can take a full breath, I sit up straighter. I look at Matt. "Alright," I say. "I have a question."

Matt takes another drink and then swallows. "Okay."

I run my hands through my hair and then cross my arms over my chest. I stare at Matt, not just his face, but like I'm giving him the once over—his chest, arms, crotch. "Tell me this," I say, looking into his eyes. "You like men?"

"Yes," he says.

"Why were you married?"

He wipes his lips with a napkin. "I'm bi," he says.

"Bi?" I say. "You're either straight, or you're gay. Bi just means you haven't figured it out yet."

"People are more complicated than that, Theo."

I look away. Jonathan presses his leg against mine under the table.

"You knew what I wanted," I say.

"No, I didn't," Matt says. "I didn't know until that night."

"You weren't interested in me?"

"Well, yes. But not for sex."

I lean back. "As a friend."

"Someone to talk to. Someone with lots of questions and an interesting point of view."

Jonathan finishes his burger. "We need to get back," he says.

"Yeah," I say. "Yeah." I eat a few more French fries. I leave money on the table. My ears pound. I walk to Jonathan's truck. It's locked. I lean against it, feeling smaller and smaller.

Jonathan waits on the steps.

"Theo," Matt says.

I'm standing on the curb, staring into the truck. "What?"

"I don't know what to do to make things okay. Do you want me to tell your parents?"

"Fuck no."

"It was my mistake, not yours. I know this isn't an excuse, but I've been fucked up since my wife left. I haven't seen my daughters in two months." He touches my elbow.

"What does that have to do with me?"

"Nothing," he says. "I've been stupid and lonely, and once it started happening, I couldn't stop. I mean, with you. At the fort." He looks into my eyes, a soft, slow look that I can't hold. "I'm so sorry," he says.

"Just be an asshole so I can hate you—"

"I *am* an asshole and you *should* hate me."

"Don't," I say. Trembling.

"I'm too old for you," Matt says.

"Why didn't you say something? The night I babysat your girls. I told you."

"I wasn't ready."

"But I told you the truth."

"Yes. But this is Missouri. I didn't expect the first young person I met to be gay."

"We've got to go," Jonathan says.

Matt nods. "Right," he says. He leans closer. "Theo, you're a great guy. I'm old. I'm fucked up," he says. "There are better guys out there for you."

I watch him leave.

Jonathan drives me back to school, silent.

I get out and put on my backpack as we walk together. The bell that ends fifth hour is ringing when the glass doors close behind us. We separate in the hallway.

I can't shake the feeling that something is wrong with me.

Seventh hour. I have walked into a cloud of blackness and inhaled deeply. Coach has his clipboard and pen in one hand, a whistle in the other, poised to blow at any time. *Blow it. Blow it like any good fag would.*

Stretching is long and slow. We are supposed to buddy up, but Donovan is absent and I am the odd man out. I stand off by myself, trying to shake out my arms and legs. I say no thanks when Coach offers to be my partner. Eberhardt is surprised, but doesn't push. A good thing. I am close to erupting.

By the time warm-up exercises are over, the final bell echoes out over the field, signaling the end of the school day. I wipe the thought of Della waiting in her dumb ass van from my head. I keep an eye on the empty stands, though, so I won't be surprised if she comes looking for me.

On my final pass around the track, I see Jonathan finding a place to sit near the edge of the bleachers. I'm on the opposite side of the field. I could exit near the locker rooms before the bend in the track. Murphy and Bryant, two teammates of the husky farm-boy type, pound the blacktop of the inside lanes. I'm lapping them. I slow down and stay behind them.

Jonathan waves. He's in sweats, a towel across his shoulders. His face is still red from soccer, and the skin close to his eye is a dark eggplant shade of purple. I stop at the fence.

"Think Coach will let you out early?"

"Doubtful," I say. I lift my shirt to wipe the sweat from my brow. Jonathan is watching.

"Let me give you a ride home."

"Della grounded me, remember? From you, the phone, my bike." I look around, scanning for her.

Eberhardt blows his whistle and calls for the team to gather around.

"Gotta go."

"I'll be in my truck," Jonathan says. "Come find me when Coach lets you out."

"Fine," I say.

The locker room is noisy, crowded with runners and soccer players and swimmers. On unlucky days like this one, the teams finish at the same time. I slide sideways to my locker, trying to take the path of least resistance. I strip in front of the wire mesh and grab my towel.

The middle showerhead of a row of nine is empty, so I turn the knob and back into the stream of water. It blasts from one unclogged nozzle, scalding heat that pierces the skin across my shoulder blades.

"Williamson!" Coach calls out.

"In the shower!" I say. I open my eyes when the last of the shampoo rinses down my face, the hot water drilling a hole in the top of my head. Coach is standing near the cinder block wall that divides the showers from the lockers.

"Della's here."

"Fuck."

"What?"

"Sorry, Coach," I say. I rinse my armpits and turn toward the nozzle to rinse my crotch while Coach waits at the edge of the wall. I shut off the water and grab my towel. "What'd she say?" I ask. I knot the towel over my hip.

"She says you'll need to be excused from the meet this weekend."

"No."

"Something about you being grounded…"

My mouth closes. I step away from the showers and lean against the painted brick wall, fighting the urge to smash my head against it.

Eberhardt shifts his clipboard and lifts his cap, wiping his face against the inside of his sleeve. "Problems at home?"

"Um, too personal to talk about here." I run my hand through my wet hair. I can't look Coach in the eye again or I'll crack into four thousand pieces.

"Theo." Eberhardt hugs the clipboard to his chest. "You don't have to work through all of this on your own."

My body nearly convulses at Coach's words. "Thanks," I say. "But I don't need any 'help' with my problem."

"Alright," Eberhardt says. "But if you need—"

"I won't."

"Well, Della's waiting for you by the stands," he says, and then he walks away.

I watch Eberhardt disappear through the fog rolling from the showers. I get dressed and exit. Not to the practice fields, but the hallway. My hope is to find Jonathan without being spotted by Della.

And I succeed. Almost. I make it to Jonathan's truck and nearly off school grounds before I catch sight of her, and she of me. "Fuck."

"You want me to stop?" Jonathan says.

"No," I say. "Yes."

"You sure?"

"Yeah."

She is walking toward us. I get out of the truck and meet her across the parking lot.

"Just what do you think you're doing?"

"I'm catching a ride."

"You weren't supposed to *be* at practice."

"Yeah, well you shouldn't be here either."

"Don't get smart with me. I told you I'd be waiting at the front entrance."

I look back at the truck. Jonathan is turned sideways, looking away. "I'm not going home with you," I say.

"I beg to differ."

"I'm not going home with you, and I'd appreciate it if you wouldn't broadcast to the world that you have a problem child."

She crosses her arms over her chest.

"You told Eberhardt, didn't you?"

"Yes."

"It's not his business!"

"Why not, Theo? Why not? You won't talk to me. You won't talk to your dad. We practically begged you to tell us if anything happened between you and Matt."

"And I told you no."

"The thing about lying, Theo, is that you usually get caught."

My hands go cold.

"Would you like to hear how I've spent my afternoon? I had to leave school early to get your dad. He called me from his office because his head hurt and he was distraught and exhausted from a conversation with Matt."

Everything in me stops.

"I suppose I should tell you what happened back in Florida, because you seem incapable of remembering."

"Don't."

"So you remember?"

"Of course I remember!" I can no longer keep my hands in my pockets. I pull my hair until it hurts. "If I were straight, you wouldn't be doing this."

She plants her hands on her hips. "Theo, if you were straight, this is *exactly* what I'd be doing. You don't seem to comprehend what he's done."

"I know what he did. I was there."

"Theo, it was wrong. It was illegal."

"It's not his fault." The words come out in a whisper. "I did it."

"Theo, *you* are the kid. *He* is the adult. He is responsible. What he did with you is illegal, Theo. He could go to jail."

"Because of me?"

"If we press charges."

"No, it was me, okay?" I wipe my palms across my face. "Okay? It was me."

She's holding her fingers to her lips, watching me.

"I made him do it."

"Theo, you might be paying for this for the rest of your life."

"God, it was just a blowjob."

"Was he wearing a condom?"

"No!"

She stands there, unmoving. "Haven't you been paying attention?"

I can't stop shaking. She goes on, telling me things I already know. She steps forward and holds my face in her hands. "This is what I wanted to protect you from, Theo. This is the big, bad world." She wraps her arms around me and holds me, trembling.

I feel so tired and small. The sun is dipping behind the trees at the edge of the practice field, low enough that it shines through strands of Della's loose hair.

"We need to get you home." She wipes a stray tear.

"I need to talk to Jonathan."

She shifts her weight, watching my face. "Alright," she says. "Five minutes."

"Fine—" I turn and run to Jonathan's truck.

He has the radio on and the windows up. He turns the music down. "How did it go?"

I can hardly breathe. "She's a crier," I say.

"I hate when parents do that shit," he says. He looks at me. "Still grounded?"

"Yeah." I wipe my cheek on my sleeve and reach for my bag. "Matt talked to my dad today and told him everything. Della says they might press charges."

"You just gave him a blowjob, right?"

I tell him yeah. I look away from him and stare at the empty parking lot with its faded stripes, the trees on the far side of the practice fields, bare branches silhouetted against a darkening blue sky. "I gotta go," I say. I slide out of the truck and close the door.

Della is waiting in the van, but she doesn't say anything when I get into the passenger seat. She doesn't say anything the entire ride, a small, kind thing for which I am very thankful.

But we don't go home. She brings me to a health clinic. At first, I refuse to get out of the car with her. She wants me to get tested for HIV, and I want her to back the hell off.

"They can test you anonymously," she says. "No one else will see the results."

"No."

"We're not leaving."

I keep saying no, and then I finally slam out of the van.

I go into a little white room with Bill, a nurse, and I decide to put my name on the form. I stare at the posters, in English and Spanish, explaining ten ways to keep me and my partner disease-free, where to call if someone I love is hurting me.

I want to say no when Bill asks if I've ever had unprotected sex. He lists all the different ways to get HIV.

"Have you ever given a blowjob?" His pen hovers above the clipboard.

"Yes."

"With or without a condom."

"Without," I say.

I can't look when the needle slides into my skin. I read about the ten ways to stay disease-free and wish I'd never met Matt. That fucking liar. If only I could go back to that night and shove him against the bricks even harder.

Usually, when I am moody, it's an angry, sick-of-the-world-and-all-its-bullshit kind of thing. The next day, though, it becomes emptiness. All is quiet in my head. No more angry dialogue.

At lunch, Jonathan says he has a plan to kidnap me. I decline his offer. There is no way I can leave the house this weekend. No phone. No track meet. No Jonathan. He is planning something for Monday. I don't care.

Something changed inside me when I saw my dad last night, after the big conversation with Matt, the crying jag in the parking lot. My old fear is back. Is Dad going to live? Is he going to die? We don't know, Theo. Am I going to live? Am I going to die? We don't know, Theo. I dream again about the stone castle.

It's like this: I find my way outside to an outdoor practice ring. There is a prince riding an animal, a horse with a bear's head. Beyond the carefully manicured ring, a tangled forest grows. I go into it, following a white stallion. It turns to me. Its left eye has been gouged out. Blood is smeared across its neck and shoulder. Its mane is long and matted with the fluid flowing from the open wound. A pony is hiding beneath the stallion, white. Its left eye is gouged out. Shivering.

My weekend is dedicated to homework, sleep, listening to music and turning over the garden for Della. By hand. It is still early spring, so the ground is heavy and damp, but I stay until the entire plot is done. I run several miles both mornings. I am quiet.

Sam checks on me in the backyard or from the hallway outside my room, trying not to be too obvious. I play a game of chess with her, and she nearly wins. If I am not moving my body, I am drifting, unable to focus.

My dad spent all of Friday in bed, the shades drawn, his head aching so that he could hardly speak. Della wants to bring him to his neurologist, but he says no, and by Saturday he is well enough to join us for dinner. Sunday night, things seem almost normal. Della and Sam laugh out loud when Dad attempts a joke and bungles the delivery. I try to laugh, too.

When Della and I are alone cleaning the dishes after dinner, she wants to talk.

"... but your father and I have the final say," she is explaining as she places a handful of sudsy utensils into my side of the sink. She doesn't like putting certain items in the dishwasher, so washing the pots and spatulas and skillets after dinner has become a ritual. One I would prefer to be left out of.

"Well?"

"What?" I say. I rinse a skillet and turn it upside down in the dish drain. I grab a towel to start drying.

"I want to know how you feel about changing some of the rules."

"What rules?" A twinge of anger shoots through my gut. It focuses my attention for a moment, on the serrated bread knife at the bottom of the sink, and then it passes. I rinse the knife and set it alongside the pans in the drain.

"… and curfew," Della says. I didn't hear the first part of her answer, but I don't bother asking. I keep rinsing and drying.

"Your father and I have been talking about helping you get in some practice time driving so you can take the test for your license. We might match your savings so you can buy a car."

"I don't want a car." My fingers squeeze around the dishtowel.

"What do you want?"

I back away from the sink, suddenly furious. I don't want to stand anywhere near her. I throw the towel onto the counter. "Okay, here's my input: I want to see Jonathan. I want my phone. I want to run track. I want you to stop telling people about my personal life."

Della rinses the last dish and shuts off the water. She turns to face me. "You're going to have to work to regain our trust."

"And how will I do that?"

She leans against the counter. "Stop the lying. That would be a good place to start. If you say you're going to be somewhere, then be there."

"But I shouldn't have to tell you where I am all the time—"

"And it's time you made some friends other than Jonathan."

"Jonathan will always be my best friend."

"Maybe, but there need to be some changes."

"Like what?"

"He's a guy. You like guys. That presents a problem."

God, I hate her. I hate her fucking logic and the pretense that she is going to include me in any decisions. "You win," I say. "You don't want my 'input.' Why don't you just tell me how it's going to be so we can get this over with?"

"Your dad and I have talked. We want things to change in a way that we can all accept." She picks up the damp dishtowel and hangs it through the drawer handle near the sink.

I watch her, wanting to leave so badly.

"This isn't easy for us. Your dad has had some difficult days—"

"Yes, I know, Della. You don't have to tell me. I already feel guilty."

She smoothes back her hair. "I appreciate that. I don't mean to make you feel any worse, but I'm getting tired of feeling like I have to protect him… from life… from you."

"Me?"

"Yes, Theo. It has been very difficult for him to deal with the recent 'revelations.' If you're sick—"

"I made a mistake—yes—but I'm not responsible for every setback of his. He doesn't need you to baby him."

"Okay," she says. "This conversation is over."

"Because you say so. Fine. I'll be waiting by the van in the morning." And I leave. I don't storm out. I walk quietly to my room, and I fume in the darkness.

CHAPTER NINE

Monday morning comes too soon. I am waiting by the van when Della and Sam come out of the house together. It's a clear, cold sunrise, and I wish I had keys so I could have gotten in and turned on the heater instead of freezing my ass off waiting.

"I didn't even know you were out here." Della clicks the remote and the doors simultaneously unlock. "Good morning," she says.

"Good morning," I say. I grab the door handle and shove my bag onto the backseat. I obey the rules, but I will not be friendly.

In front of Sam's school, Della turns in her seat and tells me to move to the front. I grab my backpack. I keep it on my lap, zipping and unzipping one of the pockets.

"Have you thought about what I said last night?"

"Yes."

"And did you come up with something you want to say about new ground rules?"

I'm tired of things always being on her terms, on her time, but I don't see many other options. "Yes," I say. "I want my phone, and I want to run track—if it's not too late."

"Dan is very understanding."

My jaw clenches, and I pull the zipper back and forth faster. "It wasn't your place to tell him about me. How would you like it if I told Jonathan about the dildos you've stockpiled since Dad's accident."

The van stops, tires screeching. "You will not talk to me like that."

"It's only fair. You seem to think it's okay to tell the whole world about me."

A car honks and she pulls over. She puts the car in park and grips the steering wheel. "Have you been going through my things?"

"No. Samantha has."

"Damn it!"

I look out the window.

"Are you lying to me? Don't pull your sister into this."

"I'm not lying. Samantha knows a lot more about your sex life than you realize."

"Why didn't you say something?"

"It's not a big deal—it's not *abnormal* for her to try to figure things out."

"Don't get sarcastic with me."

"Fine," I say. I zip my backpack closed. "I'm going to be late for school."

She takes a deep breath. "Sam has had a hard time dealing with your father's accident. I would appreciate if, in the future, you'd let me know when she does things like this."

"Okay, but I think you're overreacting."

"I know some things about your sister that you don't, and you don't need to know, but she is definitely struggling." Her voice gets quieter. "She really needs a good big brother these days."

"I *am* a good brother!" I make myself keep staring out the window so I won't say all of the mean things that are exploding in my head. I am sick of this family being in some kind of eternal recovery from Dad's stupid accident.

Della starts driving, but she is silent. For a few blocks. Then she starts up again. "Back to our earlier conversation, I will take into consideration the things you want, and maybe you, your dad, and I could talk tonight."

"Why don't you two just talk without me and let me know what you decide?"

"Don't take that attitude with me. I'm trying to be kind, and it would help if you would do the same."

"Fine," I say. I'm counting the blocks to school.

"And about your boyfriend—"

"He is not my boyfriend!"

"About Jonathan, then."

"This is not a joke. People at school don't know about either of us. You don't out someone else."

"Out?"

"Yeah, tell the world a person is gay, like you told my coach."

Finally, the school appears and she pulls into the circular front drive. "I did it because I knew you needed someone to talk to."

"It's like that test I just took—it's confidential."

"I was distraught."

"*You* were distraught. *You* needed someone to talk to. So find someone not connected to my life next time." I open the door and grab my bag. She tells me to try to have a good day.

"Yeah, you too," I say. I shut the door just short of slamming it.

Jonathan isn't in Burnett's class. He is waiting for me in the hallway afterwards.

"You missed a great class," I say. We fall into step together.

"Let's go somewhere."

"Where?"

"Away from here."

"I am seriously grounded."

"After school."

"I can't. Della will be waiting. What about lunch?"

Jonathan shifts his books and leans into me. "Can't you skip some classes?"

I look at him. His hair is poking out in tufts from under his knit cap and he hasn't shaved in days. The left eye isn't quite as swollen. It's slowly turning from purple to green and yellow around the edges. The split along his cheekbone is a small pucker of dark skin. So slow to heal. But his lip looks swollen, too.

"What happened to your lip?"

The warning bell clangs through the hallway. "Shit." He looks away. "Let's meet after lunch, okay? And then I'll get you back by the last bell."

"After 5th hour."

"Alright," he says, giving in.

I walk on a few steps, but when I turn and look back, Jonathan is already gone.

At lunch, I eat with some of the guys from the track team. The tits and ass talk isn't too bad, and I am near Stevens and Steadman. Donovan sits across from us. He is funny. Stevens and Steadman don't say much, but they laugh at Donovan's jokes about the track meet I just missed, at Donovan razzing me for letting the team down.

I dump my tray after the three of them dump theirs. We split up in the hallway, but not before Donovan gets in one last jab about me missing the meet. "Hope Coach doesn't work you too hard for not showing this weekend."

I want to say something funny, but all that comes out is *later.*

Jonathan is driving, and it's warm enough to have the windows down.

"I hope your weekend was better than mine," I say.

"I doubt it," he says. "I guess you don't know about Della calling."

"You mean she had one of her little 'talks' with your mom?

"Yeah."

"Fuck," I say. "Fucking bitch." He doesn't say anything, but I'm sure he's thinking the same thing. "Do you know what she said?"

"Enough," Jonathan answers. "Mom tried to keep it from Dad. He almost beat the shit out of me Friday night. I called my brother. He told me about this place I could stay. I haven't been home all weekend."

"You could have gone to Tom's," I say.

"I needed time alone," he says.

We ride in silence, leaving town behind and following country roads that could be leading to Jonathan's new house. But the woods look different. More fields. I don't know where we are. Jonathan slows when a meadow opens on a hill to the right.

"The house belongs to a friend of Brian's," he says. "The family used to come swimming here—there's a stream. The house is empty." His truck crests a hill, revealing a field of tall fescue, clumps bent into tufts. Patches of weeds have sprouted along the gravel tracks. Pineapple chamomile. Wood sorrel. Jonathan pulls the truck up to the house, a small bungalow with faded blue wood siding and weathered aluminum storm windows. He cuts the engine and opens his door. "Let's go see the stream," he says. He doesn't wait for my answer.

I watch him and finally get out of the truck when he disappears around the side of the house. Shit. I follow him down a path mostly overgrown with scraggly vines, Virginia creeper, Oriental bittersweet.

Finding the creek takes several minutes of walking, some of it sliding, as the path descends lower and lower. I hear the sound of water tumbling over rocks before I see the stream. It's clear, but only deeper than my knee in a few places where it gathers around fallen trees and a low bluff.

Water drips off the rock ledge, green with moss and a few maidenhair fern fiddleheads, each drop clinging to a tendril in a dark haze of green that has spread along the rock face.

"Like it?"

"Yeah," I say. "Of course." I release a slow breath, watching it blow like a plume of steam. It is cooler here by the stream bank than it was by the truck. I stand near the water's edge and pick up a twig. I snap it and then bend it between my fingers until it is broken into several pieces. Each piece ripples the water, bobbing between rocks and gravel. "How long are you going to stay here?" I select a flat rock and skip it downstream.

"I don't know."

I look at his swollen lip. "Did your dad hit you?"

"Yeah," Jonathan says. He doesn't explain any further and I don't want to push, yet.

"Come on. I want to show you something," he says. There used to be a bridge to the right, past the low bluff, and a mill. The people that owned it made moonshine. "Want to see it?" he says.

I'm looking up into the branches of the trees across the creek, noticing that the day's light doesn't seem quite so bright anymore. "It's getting late."

"Let me show you. Then we'll go."

We walk along the edge of the stream. A wall of squared stones juts halfway across the stream. Jonathan climbs up onto it and sits on the edge, his feet dangling near the water. I sit next to him.

"This is like that stone wall at Fort Pickens," I say. I run my hand along the pitted surface.

"Yeah." He throws some loose pebbles into the flowing water. "I wish I'd gone to Florida."

"Me too," I say. A lot of things would be different now.

He nods. He pulls up his knee and rests his chin. "Last week—"

"No."

"I want to say I'm sorry."

"You already did."

"I shouldn't have been there."

True. But I don't say anything.

"I'm not going to see him anymore."

"Why?"

"Because I want to be with you."

I don't speak. I gather up some sand from the wall—I tilt my palm, slowly emptying it into the water near my feet. I lean back, resting my weight on my palms. I stare up at the trees, chinquapin oak and shellbark hickory, at the patch of clouds lit bright again with sunshine. "Della called you my boyfriend this morning," I say.

Jonathan turns his head so that his cheek rests on his knee, looking at me.

My face feels warm.

"This weekend. My dad… I've had some time to think…" Jonathan doesn't finish. We are both quiet. "I want to show you the house," he says.

"I want to stay here," I say, enjoying being still and quiet for once.

"No, you're gonna love the house." Jonathan stands and pulls me with him.

The back door is open. The smell inside is close and damp, almost musty. Jonathan lights a tall candle, but it leans to the side of the cup and starts dripping.

"Here, put some wax down in the bottom," I say. I take it and let the drips pour into the cup and then press the candle into place. My stomach flutters when I hand it back to Jonathan. He leans into me and we kiss. Long, slow, and hard.

He leads me to a bedroom, holding the candle high. I sit on the bed while he undresses. I watch, unable to take my eyes away from the shadows sliding across his body as he raises both arms to pull off his shirt in the candlelight. He takes off his jeans and begins undressing me. We kiss again. I am at his neck, his ear. I tell him I want him.

He wants to know if I am sure.

Yes, I am sure. I am trembling when his lips touch my neck, collarbone, ribs, hips.

We need slippery stuff and a condom. Jonathan is prepared, but it still hurts. It always hurts the first time. Which would be okay, except that the bedspread smells like a towel that has been left in the washer too long, and I am face down. Jonathan kisses the length of my spine. I try to relax.

It does get better. Much better. Finally, even with the musty bedspread in my nose, I have an orgasm, and so does Jonathan.

"I think I just died," he says.

His body wraps around me like a second skin. "Me too," I say.

"I love you," he says, but his voice stops. A car door slams.

We both sit up in bed.

The glass on the front door shatters and the door crashes into the wall.

"Jonathan? Where the fuck are you?"

"Oh my god." Jonathan flies off the bed, pulling the bedspread with him and wrapping it around his waist. It's his dad. I grab my jeans and run after Jonathan.

"What the fuck are you doing here?"

"Getting away from you," Jonathan screams. He holds the bedspread to his chest with both hands. Dr. Norton's eyes swing from Jonathan to me. I'm still pulling on my jeans and struggling to button them. Dr. Norton closes the distance between us.

He yells at me. "You little fucker!" he says. He reaches out to grab me. Jonathan catches his dad's arm in mid-air, and Dr. Norton throws off Jonathan like he weighs nothing. Jonathan tumbles backward over the coffee table and lands on the floor, naked. Dr. Norton picks up a baseball bat lying near the front window. He swings it once against the coffee table.

I jump on him from behind as he raises the bat again. He yells, "You fucking faggot," and brings the bat down on Jonathan. It glances off his temple and rips through his shoulder. I tighten my arms around Dr. Norton's neck. I hold on despite his hand clawing at my face. He swings the bat over his head and brings it down, sweeping it across my hips. He falls back into the doorframe, slamming my body and his into the wood and broken glass of the front door.

I slump to the floor.

Jonathan is splayed between the coffee table and the sofa. Dr. Norton drops the bat and lunges toward Jonathan's neck. Jonathan kicks him in the groin, and Dr. Norton collapses on one knee beside the table.

"I'm gonna kill you," Dr. Norton says. He puts his hand on the table, trying to push to standing, but he can't move.

Jonathan shoves away the table and crawls around it, pulling me. "Let's go," he says, and we limp to the back room where Jonathan grabs his jeans and keys. We slide out through the back door as Dr. Norton is still trying to rise to his feet.

Jonathan can't move his right arm, so I have to drive. I don't know which way to go. Jonathan talks me through each turn until I recognize the streets. My left hip is aching and I am shivering. I pull slivers of glass out of my side and wipe the blood on my jeans. Jonathan is huddled against the door, his hand over his head, blood oozing through his fingers.

"We need to get you to a hospital." I touch his shoulder and he winces.

"No," he says.

"Where?"

"I don't know." His voice is dull and flat.

I drive to my house. I don't know where else to go. The van is in the driveway and Della is unloading bags from the side. She looks up when I pull in. Her first expression is fury.

Neither of us have shirts on. She sees my cuts. Then she sees Jonathan.

"He needs to go to the hospital," I say.

She sees the blood dripping from his hand. "Stay put," she says. "I'm calling an ambulance."

"Let's just drive him," I say.

"I don't know," Della yells back from the garage. "I'm calling 911."

I go around to Jonathan's door. I open it slowly. He moves, keeping himself from falling out of the truck, but he doesn't respond to my voice. Blood is soaking into his jeans and the seat of the truck. Della comes out with the portable phone.

"What happened?" she says.

"Dr. Norton hit him with a bat."

"Oh God. It looks like he's been hit on the head and the shoulder," she says into the phone. She touches Jonathan's cheek. "Jonathan?" She puts her hand on the top of his head. "He's not responding," she says into the phone. "Go get some towels and a blanket," she says to me. "Okay. I'll stay on the line." She looks at me. "Theo. Get some towels and a blanket."

"Is he okay?"

"They're sending an ambulance." She pulls me from him. "I'll stay with him."

I run into the house, and when I come back, the sirens are already a few streets away. Jonathan still isn't responding to Della. She holds the phone between her ear and her shoulder. She places the towels gently on Jonathan's chest and near his head. She tucks the blanket around him and tells me to wrap the other blanket around myself.

I ride in the ambulance sitting on a bench seat while a paramedic wipes my cuts. Jonathan is on a stretcher, his neck in a brace, his eyes closed. Della holds his hand and leans over him, telling him everything is going to be okay. I close my eyes, remembering how good Della is at comforting the wounded.

Jonathan has a concussion and a broken collarbone. His dad is under house arrest, and Jonathan's mom stays the first night in the hospital. She is afraid to go home.

"I have to get clean clothes for him," Mrs. Norton tells Della on the second day. But Mrs. Norton doesn't come back.

I bring pajamas for him. He's not awake yet, and I can't stand the sounds the little machine makes. I go home with Dad and Della. She asks later if I want to go back with her, to bring him flowers.

"No," I say. "I have homework."

In my room, I put on my headphones and push in the CD I've listened to so many times in the past few weeks. When it gets to track ten, I push the button to repeat the song and get out the liner notes. I scan the tiny print and catch something I've never noticed before. "...these three cubic feet of bone and blood and meat are all I love and know/ 'Cause I'm a one man guy." And it isn't even written by Rufus. It's his dad's song. All this time, I've thought Rufus was singing about being in love with only one guy at a time. But his dad, Loudon Wainwright III, is seriously straight. And seriously an asshole. This song means something different.

My head empties and I can feel the ache in my hip where Dr. Norton hit me, the pull of scabs along my ribs.

I realize Rufus is singing about being your own guy, not being someone else's guy. I lie on my bed, huddled, the song repeating over and over. I bury my face in my pillow.

Della pushes open my door.

"Get out!" I scream at her.

"Theo."

"No," I say. "Go away."

She sits on the edge of my bed. She pulls off the headphones. "Theo, they're going to let Jonathan out soon," she says.

"So."

"He can't go home." She pulls up the cover over my shoulder.

"He can go live with Brian," I say.

"Okay," she says. "Okay." And she leaves.

On the next day, the third day, Jonathan is awake. Dad gives him a bar of chocolate, fingers trembling as he sets it on the little wheeled table.

"We can't stay long," Dad says.

Della holds Jonathan's hand.

I sit on the window seat, staring at his head bandages. He turns to look at me, and I can't meet his eyes.

"We'll be back tomorrow," Della says.

In a few days, he is ready to leave the hospital. Mrs. Norton has called Della to tell her Jonathan's brother Brian will become his guardian. Della is stunned.

We pick up Jonathan from the hospital, and I feel sick. Both of his eyes are bruised. The one on the right, where his dad hit him with the bat, is deep purple and blue, swollen. His left eye, where I punched him, is a kaleidoscope of green and yellow.

He stays with us one night before he takes the bus to Brian's house in Columbia. He sleeps in the guest room. I lie on my bed, breathing too fast, listening to Wainwright's track 10 again and again. And then I understand.

It's like getting a joke a day later, or a month, or a lifetime.

It's like this: three cubic feet of flesh and blood and bone is all we get, in this life. The joke is that you can either love someone or not love someone, but in this life, our body, our little bit of space that we get to occupy, is it. There is no choice about living in a body that can be broken and bruised. Bloodied. This is all we get. But there is a choice to love. Or not.

I stand, my eyes sore from crying. I go to Jonathan's room.

"What?" he says. The light on the bedside table is dim. He is staring at it.

"I'm sorry," I say.

"It was my fault," he says. "I wasn't good for you."

"It's your dad's fault," I say.

Jonathan looks at me.

"You kept telling me no because of him." I sit on the end of the bed.

"I told you no because I didn't love you."

Something catches in my chest. "No," I say. "Stop trying to protect me." I lean forward and crawl up the bed to his body. He watches me come. "All those stories," I say. "All those men you blew or fucked. I don't believe it."

He puts his hand up to stop me from getting closer. "Don't," he says.

"So you fucked them. So you fucked Tom." I move closer to his face. "I don't care."

"Don't."

I take his hand and hold it. I look at the bandage on his head, his swollen eye and cheekbone, and my heart is pounding. "I love you, and you're not taking that away from me." I am crying. I kiss his hand, and he squeezes his eyes shut.

"Please go," he says.

"Let me stay," I say.

He pulls my hand to his chest.

I settle in beside him, my arm draped across his body, and then we finally fall asleep together.

Many thanks to...

The University of Missouri Creative Writing Program and Vermont Studio Center. Marly, Trudy, Maureen, Andy, Heather, and Speer. Andrew, Lily, Mike, and Anthony. Joy, Aisha, Brad, Hoyt, Sierra, Ben, Corey, Cody, Elizabeth, Kyna, Roxane, Letitia, Jeanne, and Davina.
Joel and Daniel.
Jeff.